ACES HEROES and DAREDEVILS of the AIR

In these pages you will meet the daring fliers of the first four decades of flight. Some flew their fragile planes for fun, indulging in acrobatics in the sky. Daredevil Cal Rodgers set a record flying across the country in seven weeks in his jaunty plane, the *Vin-Fiz Flyer*, followed by a private train stocked with supplies. In World War I the famous Red Baron, Billy Bishop, and the American fliers known as the Lafayette Escadrille caught the world's attention with their brave air battles. Heroics in the air continued in peacetime and in the desperate air battles of World War II. Flying attracts the adventurous and their stories make exciting reading.

Also by LeRoy Hayman

Thirteen Who Vanished

Up, Up, and Away
All About Balloons, Blimps, and Dirigibles

ACES HEROES and DAREDEVILS of the AIR

LeRoy Hayman

Photographs

Julian Messner New York

Copyright © 1981 by LeRoy Hayman

All rights reserved including the right of
reproduction in whole or in part in any form.
Published by Julian Messner, a Simon & Schuster
Division of Gulf & Western Corporation,
Simon & Schuster Building,
1230 Avenue of the Americas,
New York, New York 10020
JULIAN MESSNER and colophon are trademarks of
Simon & Schuster, registered in the U.S. Patent
and Trademark Office.

Manufactured in the United States of America.

Design by Irving Perkins Associates

Library of Congress Cataloging in Publication Data

Hayman, LeRoy.
Aces, heroes, and daredevils of the air.

  Bibliography: p.
  Includes index.
  Summary: Highlights the exploits of the men and women involved in four decades of aviation beginning with the Wright brothers' flight in 1903 through the flight of the B-29 that carried the atomic bomb to Japan in 1945.
  1. Air pilots—Biography—Juvenile literature.
[1. Air pilots. 2. Aeronautics—History] I. Title.
TL539.H32   629.13′092′2 [920]   81-2235
ISBN 0-671-34049-2   AACR2

To all my shipmates aboard
the U.S.S. *PC-490* (1943–1944) and
the U.S.S. *Arkansas* (1944–1945)

My special thanks to Elaine Buller, who threaded her way through the Washington maze in hot pursuit of the pictures for this book.

Photos: National Archives

Contents

INTRODUCTION 9

CHAPTER

1. *BUILDING AND FLYING THE FIRST ONES* THE WRIGHT BROTHERS, GLENN CURTISS 11

2. *THE SHORT, HAPPY (?) LIVES OF TWO DAREDEVILS* CALBRAITH PERRY RODGERS, LINCOLN BEACHEY   23

3. *A DUTCH DESIGNER AND A GERMAN ACE OF ACES* ANTHONY FOKKER, MANFRED VON RICHTHOFEN (THE RED BARON) 34

4. *TWO BRITISH ACES* ALBERT BALL, BILLY BISHOP 45

5. *THREE FRENCH FLIERS* ROLAND GARROS, GEORGES GUYNEMER, RENÉ FONCK 56

6. *A SALUTE TO LAFAYETTE* 67

7.	**AMERICAN ACES IN WORLD WAR I** FRANK LUKE, EDDIE RICKENBACKER..........................	**75**
8.	**MITCHELL AND THE FIGHT FOR AIR FORCE RECOGNITION**	**87**
9.	**FLYING THE ATLANTIC** ALCOCK/BROWN, CHARLES LINDBERGH	**99**
10.	**TO AUSTRALIA, THEN AROUND THE WORLD** ROSS SMITH, CHARLES KINGSFORD-SMITH, WILEY POST	**111**
11.	**THE BATTLE OF BRITAIN** DOUGLAS BADER.......................	**124**
12.	**DOOLITTLE'S RAIDERS AND BOYINGTON'S BLACK SHEEP**	**133**
13.	**DAUNTLESS WOMEN OF THE AIR** AMELIA EARHART, JACQUELINE COCHRAN, HANNA REITSCH	**147**
14.	**DESTROYING HITLER'S INDUSTRIAL MIGHT** GUY GIBSON.......	**158**
15.	**PILOTS OF THE DIVINE WIND** ...	**166**
16.	**DESTRUCTION FROM THE SKIES**	**175**
	BIBLIOGRAPHY	**183**
	INDEX	**186**

Introduction

Welcome to the world of fliers! In this book you'll meet a host of men and women who made aviation their career, their lifelong passion. They built planes or piloted them in peace or in war, in transatlantic flights or around the world, in dogfights against enemy aircraft or in bombing raids on enemy targets.

Aces, Heroes, and Daredevils of the Air is not an encyclopedia of aviation. It is a collection of accounts full of the excitement of flying. It begins with the first flight of the Wright brothers in 1903 and ends with the B-29 flight that carried out the atomic bombing of Japan in 1945.

Within these first four decades of flight countless valiant airmen and airwomen undertook great challenges, often in airplanes that were fragile and untested. Their stories will give you a good idea of the bravery, the achievement, the sacrifice of people who devoted their lives to aviation.

What does the book's title mean? *Aces* is a World War I term, meaning a pilot who had downed at least five enemy planes. The word *hero* has the less exact meaning of a courageous person who does brave deeds. Here it applies to the men and women who did fine things in aviation, sometimes at the cost of their lives. A *daredevil* is a person who takes great risks to put on a good air show. Each of the fliers you'll meet in this book fits under at least one of these names, perhaps even under two or three.

You may have been a passenger in a giant airliner or in a small private plane. Or you may have not yet been aloft at all. No matter. If the sight of an aircraft coursing steadily through the sky thrills you, then this book is for you.

—LeRoy Hayman

CHAPTER 1
BUILDING AND FLYING THE FIRST ONES
THE WRIGHT BROTHERS, GLENN CURTISS

It was a cold, windy day on the Atlantic Ocean beach near Kitty Hawk, North Carolina. The date was December 17, 1903, just a few days before the winter solstice, the shortest day of the year. Two men stood silent before a sprawling, rickety-looking contraption perched on its wooden launching rail. A few spectators, four men and a boy, watched them intently, waiting to see if the contraption would work.

The Brothers Wright

THE TWO men were Orville and Wilbur Wright, and their contraption was a flying machine—an airplane complete with an engine and a place for a pilot—designed to move through the skies under its own power. The plane was called the *Flyer*, and this was the day the Wright brothers were going to fly their *Flyer*. Men had already gone aloft in balloons, dirigibles, and gliders, but no one had yet taken to the air successfully in a powered, heavier-than-air craft.

Both in their thirties, the Wrights were two of the five children of a bishop of the United Brethren Church in Dayton, Ohio. Milton Wright had taught his sons to work hard and save their money—but he didn't mind seeing them spend their earnings on flight experiments.

Neither Wilbur nor Orville ever finished high school, and both were to be lifelong bachelors. Eleven years before this session at Kitty Hawk, they had gone into the bicycle business. They assembled, sold, and repaired two-wheelers and built some custom-tailored bikes themselves.

To look at the Wright brothers in those days, you'd never have guessed that soon they would launch one of the most important industries of the twentieth century. They were neat, small, quiet men, both growing bald, who kept pretty much to themselves. They'd been fascinated by the idea of aviation ever since they had flown kites as boys. Growing up, they read about the glider experiments of Otto Lilienthal and Octave Chanute and decided to construct some gliders of their own.

Their first product was a *biplane* (double-wing) glider kite. It had a new feature that they later built into the *Flyer*. This was *wing-warping*, a way of bending the wings, especially in a turn, to make best use of the air flowing over them.

With the success of the biplane glider, the Wrights were in the experimental aircraft business to stay. They wrote the U.S. Weather Bureau to learn where the strongest, steadiest winds blew. They needed such winds to support their gliders in the air. The bureau told them about the Carolina coast.

So in the fall of 1900 the brothers were on the beach at Kitty Hawk with a new manned glider with warped wings and with an elevator in front for better up-and-down movement. Testing the wing warping and the elevator, they made several good glider flights. Either Orville or Wilbur acted as glider pilot.

It was back to Kitty Hawk a year later, this time with a bigger glider they were counting on. Sad to say, the new glider flew poorly. On their return to Dayton, they set up a wind tunnel to test the data provided by glider pioneers Lilienthal and Chanute. The tests showed that Lilienthal's and Chanute's facts and figures were wrong. Because of the wrong data, the new glider needed redesigning.

In 1902 they were again in Kitty Hawk. This year's glider had straighter wings, a movable rudder, and better control of the wing warping. They made more than a thousand flights off the lonely beaches.

Glider flights were fine in their way, but they were self-limiting. A glider pilot depended on steady winds, and when these died down, he went down. After their glider successes, the Wrights were ready to think about powered flight. They had to consider two new elements: an engine and a propeller.

The engine had to be light and powerful for its size. The brothers tried to buy an engine that would fit their needs, but none was on the market. So in the winter of 1902–1903 they built their own. The gasoline engine was square, with four cylinders that produced twelve horsepower and weighed 152 pounds. Its speed was a little more than a thousand revolutions per minute.

14/ ACES, HEROES, AND DAREDEVILS OF THE AIR

Nor was there any airplane propeller to be bought. As they had done with the engine, the Wrights designed and built their own propeller. They actually built two, which they installed behind the engine and behind the pilot. A bicycle chain attachment carried power back from engine to propellers. Located in the rear, the props "pushed" the plane forward.

At Kitty Hawk in the fall of 1903 the Wrights ran into trouble with their new engine and propellers. Patiently they solved each problem, corrected each fault. On De-

Orville and Wilbur Wright and unidentified friend make last minute flight adjustments to the Wright *Flyer* of 1908.

cember 14 Wilbur tried to take off in the *Flyer*. The plane scooted along the launching track and started to climb. Almost at once the engine stalled, and the *Flyer* belly-flopped on the beach.

On December 17 the Wrights were ready to try again. This time Orville climbed into *Flyer* and lay belly down on the lower wing. He started the engine, and the craft moved forward along the rail. Then it took off into the wind and flew for twelve seconds, covering 120 feet.

It was done. The human race was no longer earthbound. We had conquered the air.

That day the Wrights made three more flights, the last one for a distance of 852 feet in 59 seconds. Orville sent a telegram to their father: "Success four flights Thursday morning all against 21-mile wind started from level with engine power alone average speed through air 31 miles longest 59 seconds inform press home Christmas."

It was the merriest Christmas the Wrights were ever to have. The years ahead would bring many disappointments. Even though they had wired Milton Wright to "inform press," the modest brothers did not know how to take advantage of their accomplishment. Nor did they especially want to. For several years the newspapers ignored their achievement. Even the most important magazine of its kind, *Scientific American*, did not recognize the Wrights and their revolutionary invention until 1906. That same year the Wrights were granted patents on their plane.

Competitor to the Wrights

ABOUT THIS time a strong competitor of the Wright brothers made his entrance onto the aviation scene. He was Glenn Curtiss, a self-taught engineer, who would later become a record-setting pilot and developer of the Jenny, the workhorse plane of flying's early days.

Like the Wrights, Glenn Curtiss was at first a bicycle dealer. Before he was twenty, the sign on his Hammondsport, New York, shop read: "G.H. CURTISS, DEALER IN HARNESS AND HORSE FURNISHINGS, ALSO BICYCLES AND SUNDRIES." Harness may have been the leading item on his sign, but he did his biggest business in bikes.

Young Curtiss married at twenty-one. His bride was Lena Neff, eighteen, a local girl. In later years Lena was to say that she always trusted Glenn, yet always feared for his life when he raced his new and untested aircraft.

After the wedding, G.H. (as the Hammondsport people were beginning to call him) concentrated on turning out better two-wheelers. Soon he was working on motorized bikes. For his first, he built his own engine and his own carburetor, an old tomato can covered by a gauze screen. The rear wheel was driven by a belt running back from the engine.

In a short time Curtiss was building bigger and better motorcycles. Hammondsport businessmen knew that G.H. was onto something good and set up a little motorcycle factory in town for him. To promote his vehicles, G.H. raced them in national meetings. In 1903 he won the gold medal in the National Cycling Association race and was named national champion.

The motorcycle factory was turning out scores of vehicles, but cash wasn't coming in as fast as it should. A Californian named Thomas Scott Baldwin saw the Curtiss motorcycle engine and wanted one for a new dirigible he was building. Baldwin ordered the engine, and when delivery was stalled, he went to Hammondsport to find out why. Curtiss had slowed production because he lacked money.

Baldwin supplied the needed cash and got his engine promptly.

Baldwin gave full credit to Curtiss for the success of his *California Arrow* dirigible. "It was the motor," he said. "The *California Arrow* could not have flown without it." Baldwin was to prove a staunch friend in the critical years ahead.

In 1906 Baldwin was flying his dirigible in Dayton, Ohio. Engine repairs were needed, and G.H. came down to Dayton to do the work. Baldwin introduced him to Orville and Wilbur Wright, who turned out to be friendly folks—the bitter rivalry between the Wrights and Curtiss was in the future. The Wrights talked freely and showed Curtiss several photos of their *Flyer*. They would not, however, show him the plane itself.

The next year Curtiss was in Ormond Beach, Florida, fitting a new engine into one of Baldwin's dirigibles. G.H. had taken along a new motorcycle with radical design features. He decided to give this vehicle a speed trial. Under test conditions he drove the cycle for a measured mile on the beach. Curtiss racked up a record of 26.4 seconds for the distance, a speed of 136.3 miles per hour. Newspapers all over the country headlined him as the "Fastest Man on Earth."

All this is prologue to the dramatic story of Glenn Curtiss and aviation. That story began when Dr. Alexander Graham Bell, famous for his invention of the telephone, met G.H. at the 1906 Aero Club show in New York. On display was a Curtiss engine, like the ones used in the Baldwin dirigibles. Dr. Bell had made many experiments in kite flying; now he wanted to install an engine in a man-carrying kite. He ordered one from Curtiss, and when it wasn't delivered, he—like Baldwin—came to

Hammondsport to ask the reason for the delay. Bell's visit resulted in a firm friendship with Curtiss.

Later, at Bell's estate in Nova Scotia, Canada, Curtiss met three young flying enthusiasts: Frederick W. "Casey" Baldwin (no relation to the dirigible captain), John A. D. McCurdy, and Lieutenant Thomas E. Selfridge, U. S. Army. The first two were college-trained engineers. Selfridge, a West Point graduate, was on leave to help Bell with his kite experiments.

The five soon agreed to form the Aerial Experiment Association (AEA). Its purpose: to design and build a self-powered aircraft, capable of carrying a person. They knew, of course, of the Wright brothers' work, but they were determined to go their own way, avoiding infringement on the Wrights' 1906 airplane patents.

The AEA group began building *Drome No. 1*, nicknaming it *Red Wing* from the red silk used on its wings. They had very little to go on by way of design models or research data. In fact, Selfridge wrote to ask the Wrights how to build wings and attach fabric to cover them. The Wrights wrote back with full explanations and references to journals that had published their data. They also told Selfridge to look up their 1906 patents.

Red Wing was a biplane powered by a Curtiss air-cooled engine. It had eight cylinders and could generate up to forty horsepower. The steel propeller was driven directly off the engine; no belt was used. Since it was to be tested on the ice of Keuka Lake, near Hammondsport, it was mounted on wooden runners, not wheels.

On its first test, with Casey Baldwin as pilot, *Red Wing* rose to a height of six or eight feet and flew a distance of 318 feet before it was forced down on the ice. On its next flight *Red Wing* crashed at once. It was a total wreck.

Next came *Drome No. 2*, nicknamed *White Wing*. The big difference between *No. 1* and *No. 2* was in the use of ailerons. The hinged ailerons, located at the outer edges of the wings, could be tipped to change the angle of the wind flow and thus keep the plane itself from going off course while in level flight. The ailerons were Dr. Bell's idea.

White Wing was flight-tested by Casey Baldwin, Selfridge, Curtiss, and McCurdy. None was able to keep the plane aloft for more than nineteen seconds or travel much farther than a thousand feet. On its last flight, with Jack McCurdy as pilot, *White Wing* crashed and was damaged beyond repair.

Up to this time Curtiss had worked mainly on the aircraft engines, keeping them in good running order. But he had held back somewhat because he was perhaps overly impressed by the background and credentials of his AEA associates. Dr. Bell was a world-famous inventor; Baldwin and McCurdy were graduate engineers; Tom Selfridge was an army officer.

But G.H. had never gone beyond the first year of high school, and he had built his motorcycle business from scratch. The AEA work required a knowledge of airplane theory and design, and Curtiss felt shy. In time, however, he learned to work with the others and was considered one of them.

Drome No. 3, or *June Bug*, was the group's third and best plane thus far. It had improved ailerons that prevented unwanted tips and turns. Curtiss was given the task of piloting all of *June Bug*'s flights. The group decided that too many pilot cooks would spoil the airplane's broth.

After a series of test flights, Curtiss decided that *June Bug* was ready to try for the *Scientific American* trophy. This prize was to be awarded to the first plane that flew a distance of one kilometer (3,180 feet, or about six-tenths of a mile) in a straight line. The flight had to be made under official conditions and witnessed by the public.

One reason that the *Scientific American* offered the prize was the hope that the Wright brothers would come out of hiding and show the public their plane. Ever since their 1903 flight the Wrights had remained in seclusion, keeping their tests and trials secret from the scientific world and the general public. Despite the lure of the $2,500 prize that went with the trophy, the Wrights still kept to themselves. Glenn Curtiss was the first to apply for a test.

The contest rules stated the the prize-seeker could name his own place for the trials. G.H. chose Hammondsport, and the Aero Club, which conducted the tests, had to agree to the location. So the Aero Club officials and observers trekked 300 miles from New York City to upstate Hammondsport on July 4, 1908, to judge the *June Bug*.

Also on hand were farm families from the whole Finger Lakes area, in a holiday mood, ready to watch their local boy, Glenn Curtiss, make a prize-winning flight. A covey of newsmen was there to see if the former motorcycle champion would earn new fame as a pioneer airplane pilot.

The test site was the town's racetrack. Judges, reporters, and visitors assembled to watch G.H. try for the trophy. On his first attempt, Curtiss failed, but his second try was successful. He covered 5,090 feet—1,810 feet more than was required. Aero Club officials and local farmers roared their approval. Everyone sensed that aviation history was made on that festive Fourth of July.

But right after G.H.'s aerial triumph, he received a letter from Orville Wright containing a charge that was to drag on for years. Wright stated that Curtiss's ailerons were nothing more than the wing-warping feature fully protected by the Wrights' 1906 airplane patents. The Wrights sued and finally won. However, all future planes used ailerons, so the Wrights' victory was an empty one.

In the fall of 1908 the Wright brothers were demonstrating their craft before a group of army observers. Among them was Lieutenant Tom Selfridge, who probably knew more about airplanes than anyone else in the army.

On the final test Selfridge went up in the airplane with Orville Wright. The Wright *Flyer* circled the field four times before something went amiss. The plane came down swiftly and crashed into the dust. Orville suffered severe hip, leg, and rib injuries, but recovered after seven weeks in the hospital. Selfridge was pulled out of the wreck alive, but died some hours later. He was only twenty-six. It was later found that a crack in the propeller had caused the crash.

Mourning the loss of Selfridge, the AEA kept on for a while. It built a fourth plane, *Silver Dart*, and flew it many times to chalk up a record total of more than a thousand miles. On his own, Curtiss attached pontoons to the old *June Bug* for takeoffs and landings on Keuka Lake. But he could never get up enough speed to overcome the suction of the water on the pontoons. It was good experience, however, for his later work with the U. S. Navy.

Without Selfridge, the AEA finally began to disintegrate. Dr. Bell flew his kites up a blind alley. Casey Baldwin and Jack McCurdy in time gave up flying altogether. G.H. was the only active one left.

In the meantime the Wright brothers kept busy. Even before the Selfridge crash, they had won a U.S. government contract to build a plane for the army. Seeking another contract, Wilbur sailed for France, his disassembled *Flyer* in the ship's hold. Landing, he proceeded to Le Mans.

There he flew distances of twelve miles or more, captivating the press and public with his sure touch on the aircraft controls. The French, who had pioneered in lighter-than-air craft, were delighted with Wilbur Wright. After he returned home, Wilbur helped Orville turn out the U.S. Army's first plane.

For his part Glenn Curtiss went into the airplane manufacturing business with Augustus Herring, who had once worked with the Wrights. In his new *Gold Bug*, G.H. won a second *Scientific American* trophy. Then he quickly journeyed to France to fly in the widely advertised meet at Rheims. He was the only American in the contest, and a number of Europe's great pilots were flying against him. Curtiss won the coveted Gordon Bennett speed trophy, racking up an average 47 miles per hour over a 20 kilometer course.

Even sweeter was Curtiss's 1910 achievement. He won the New York *World* newspaper prize of $10,000 by flying 142 miles along the Hudson River from Albany, New York, to New York City. He stopped twice to refuel.

For this event thousands of New Yorkers thronged rooftops and other open places where they could look up and see Glen Curtiss's plane winging through the sky. Few of these thousands had ever seen any kind of airplane before. For them and for the other millions who could only read about the flight, Glenn Curtiss became America's first air hero.

CHAPTER
THE SHORT, HAPPY (?) LIVES OF TWO DAREDEVILS
CALBRAITH PERRY RODGERS, LINCOLN BEACHEY

During the last few years before the start of World War I in 1914, people were generally optimistic. "We're living in the best of times since history began," they said.

In the United States most workers were earning a decent living. The prices of food, clothing, and shelter were not out of reach for most people. The majority of children were in school, although some children still labored long hours on farms or in mines and factories. Land was still cheap, and if a man couldn't succeed in the East, he could always pick himself up and go out West.

Cities and towns were laying down paved streets for the new automobiles, and highways were replacing the old rutted roads that ran between communities. Long-distance telephone lines provided other links between separated families and friends. Electric power lines were beginning to reach out to serve farms. The signs of progress were everywhere.

But nothing spelled out "progress" more dramatically than that new invention, the airplane. Not many people had actually seen an airplane overhead, but everyone was talking about "aeroplanes," as the word was spelled then.

Imagine, people said, a pilot can just get into his plane and fly thousands of feet into the clouds! Or he can fly cross-country for dozens of miles in dozens of minutes! It was incredible, unheard of, amazing—but the airplane was here, and here to stay. It wasn't long before "Come, Josephine, in My Flying Machine" became a leading popular tune.

After the international aviation meet in Rheims, France, in 1909, the one starring Glenn Curtiss, came many more. In 1910 the United States staged air competitions on both coasts. At Los Angeles a speed record of 55 miles per hour was set by a plane carrying pilot and passenger. At Boston a Curtiss team pilot set a duration record of more than three hours in the air. A Wright-sponsored flier set an altitude record of 4,732 feet. An Englishman, Claude Grahame-White, won a $10,000 prize by racing around Boston Light in record time: 33 miles in just over 34 minutes. At Belmont Park, on New York's Long Island, Grahame-White set two more speed records.

Wilbur Wright died unexpectedly in 1912, but Orville carried on alone. More government contracts made him quietly prosperous. Glenn Curtiss developed seaplanes for the U. S. Navy, as well as a plane that could take off and land on the built-up stern of a battleship. This development was the first step toward the modern aircraft carrier. Curtiss was also hard at work on his Jennys, planes that would later serve as training vehicles for student pilots in World War I.

This prewar period, when aviation was in its infancy,

also had its lunatic fringe. Call them what you will—daredevils, kooks, crackpots—these bold and fearless fliers made headlines with their aerial feats and stunts. They risked their lives in their spit-and-bailing-wire craft to please the crowds that gathered on bright weekend afternoons to watch the spectacles—and the crackups.

Bud Mars, the Curtiss Daredevil

YOUNG J.C. MCBRIDE began his working career as a newsboy. But delivering papers and sometimes selling them on street corners proved too slow for the boy. He was soon a member of a vaudeville act that toured the small towns of the Middle West. Even this life did not provide the adventure he needed.

So when he was fifteen he changed his name to Bud Mars and joined a circus as tumbler and acrobat. Again, the circus life was not highly charged enough, so he became a high diver. He dove from tall towers into shallow pools, risk enough to satisfy any other daredevil.

But the risk was too small to suit Bud Mars. He became a parachutist, jumping from hot air balloons and landing right in the midst of farmers attending a county or state fair.

Hot air balloons led to airplanes. In 1909 Glenn Curtiss taught Bud Mars how to fly. At last Mars found a way to satisfy his hunger for thrills and applause. Bud Mars spent the rest of his days in aviation, the early years of which were devoted to stunt flying.

Bud Mars and his plane went back to the fairgrounds with a series of stunts that dazzled the crowds. In the air he would loop, barrel-roll, and perform all the other tricks that seem so spectacular even now. Then, before landing, he would circle the field and watch the fair officials try to shoo the spectators away in order to make space for him to come down.

All of a sudden he would point the plane's nose at the crowds and come barreling down for what had to be a crash landing in their midst. At the last possible moment he'd pull out of the dive, circle the field, and come down safely. There would always be a landing space left for him by the now-fearful spectators. For such daredevil feats, Bud Mars earned as much as $5,000 in a single Sunday afternoon.

In 1914 he almost died after flying an exhibition at Erie, Pennsylvania. Bud Mars crash-landed; his plane was destroyed and he was crushed by the wreckage. But he lived. And more, he became a flight instructor in the Air Service in World War I and continued flying for the rest of his days.

Flying Coast to Coast

MANY DAREDEVILS were in the American skies during Bud Mars' stunting days, but one man's zany flight bears a closer look. The man was Calbraith Perry Rodgers.

Rodgers's forebears had helped make American history. One great-uncle was Commodore Oliver Hazard Perry, remembered for his famous announcement, "We have met the enemy, and they are ours!" made on Lake Erie during the War of 1812. Rodgers's grandfather was Commodore Matthew Calbraith Perry, who opened Japan to world trade in 1853, and his father was an army officer who was killed during an Indian uprising. Cal Rodgers himself was turned down by the U.S. Naval Academy because of partial deafness.

So Cal Rodgers, all six feet four of him, enrolled at New York's Columbia University and became a football star. Family money enabled him to become a full-time sportsman after college. As such he raced yachts, autos, and horses.

Rodgers was a young married man in 1911 when he decided to race the fastest vehicle of all, the airplane. Actually he knew little about flying when he made this decision. Nevertheless he entrained to Dayton, Ohio, where he signed up for flying lessons with the Wright brothers. He soon established his identification mark: a cold, half-smoked cigar clenched between his teeth whenever he was in the air.

As soon as Rodgers learned to fly, he bought a plane from the Wrights. In it he won an endurance record prize of $11,000 at a Chicago air meet in 1911—even though his log showed a previous record of only a few hours in the air.

With the $11,000 in his pocket, Rodgers made up his mind to win the biggest aviation prize then being offered: the $50,000 put up by newspaper tycoon William Randolph Hearst for the first flier to make it from coast to coast by air in thirty days. Trouble was, the offer expired on October 11, 1911, and here it was already August. The latest Rodgers could start and still have thirty days was September 11.

And much remained to be done. Rodgers had money, but he did not care to finance the whole—and very expensive—flight. In 1911 a pilot could not simply get into his plane in New York and fly nonstop to Los Angeles. Even the best pilots rarely flew more than a hundred miles or so before they set their planes down for refueling and repairs. There weren't many places across the United States where a pilot could land and get such service.

The only answer to Rodgers's problem was a train that would follow the plane across the country. Its cars would carry gasoline, a repair shop, sleeping quarters for pilot and ground crew, a diner, and so on. All this would be costly, and Rodgers needed a backer to bear the expense.

He found one in J. Ogden Armour, the Chicago meat-packing millionaire. Armour was getting ready to market a new soft drink called Vin-Fiz, and he was looking for a way to publicize the name. The two struck a bargain. Rodgers was to furnish the plane, on which the name Vin-Fiz would be painted in big, bold letters. Armour was to pay Rodgers three dollars for every mile the plane flew on its transcontinental route. Rodgers was to pay the cost of repairs along the way out of the three-dollars-a-mile fee.

Best of all, Armour was to pay for the train. The train turned out to be something special. Each car was emblazoned with the name Vin-Fiz. A sleeping car housed Rodgers's wife, mother, doctor, manager, three mechanics, and a chauffeur. The repair car held tools, enough spare parts to build a whole new plane, gasoline, oil, a tow truck, and Rodgers's sports car.

Rodgers bought a new plane from the Wrights, who also lent him their top mechanic for the trip. Time rushed by, and it was not until September 17 that Rodgers was ready to begin his flight. Only twenty-five days remained before the Hearst offer was to expire.

Rodgers took off from Sheepshead Bay in Brooklyn in the afternoon and flew to Middletown, New York, a distance of eighty miles in 115 minutes. "So far this is easy," he probably said to himself. "I'll do one hop in the morning, one in the afternoon, and make it in fifteen days."

THE SHORT, HAPPY (?) LIVES OF TWO DAREDEVILS / 29

It was a different story the next morning. Caught in the tricky winds of the Catskill Mountains, Rodgers's plane tangled with the treetops. He crash-landed into a chicken coop, smashing the landing skid of the plane and cracking a wing. Rodgers suffered cuts and bruises and a wrenched knee. It took the mechanics three days to repair the plane, now officially named the *Vin-Fiz Flyer*. There were twenty-one days left.

The next day he made it to Binghamton, still in New York State. He landed in a field outside town and left the plane in search of a telephone. While he was gone, souvenir-hunters swarmed all over the *Vin-Fiz Flyer*. They grabbed everything that could be pried loose, especially nuts and bolts in the engine.

The results of the scavenging soon became apparent. On the way from Elmira to Salamanca, the *Vin-Fiz Flyer*'s engine began to knock, the propeller to spin more slowly. Rodgers soon saw that the magneto plugs were slipping out.

What to do? Rodgers put one hand on the plugs, shut off the motor, and glided to earth 2,600 feet below. Landing in a swamp, he damaged the lower wings. The mechanics worked on the plane all night, and Rodgers started off for Salamanca in the morning. Now there were only seventeen days left.

Attempting to take off that afternoon, Rodgers misjudged distances and flew into a barbed-wire fence. Another three days were consumed in making repairs.

On his way to Akron, Rodgers got lost. The moon came up—this was the first time he had flown at night—and he landed in a cow pasture near Kent, Ohio. The cows fled, but Rodgers felt he had to stay with his plane all night. He feared that the Kent cows might do the same stripping job that the Binghamton souvenir-seekers had done.

After another day's delay he headed for Huntington, Indiana. He ran into a thunderstorm that turned him miles off his heading. Finally making it to Huntington, he was met by an enthusiastic and seemingly uncontrollable crowd. People swarmed all over Rodgers and the *Vin-Fiz Flyer*, shaking his hand, holding up their babies to be kissed. When he tried to take off, a mob stood directly in front of his plane. To avoid hitting (and hurting) his well-wishers, he turned the plane's nose into a fence. The result: an almost total wreck.

His crew accomplished a miraculous rebuilding job. Two days later he was off to Chicago. It was now October 8, and the Hearst deadline was October 11. It was impossible to get in under the wire, even though Rodgers had already flown 1,272 miles, a new cross-country record. Next major stop: Kansas City, Missouri, the halfway point between New York and California.

There Rodgers bade an official good-bye to the Hearst prize. But he had no intention of discontinuing his transcontinental trip. He still wanted to be the first man to fly from coast to coast in one sustained effort. Relieved of the deadline pressure, Rodgers now set out to please the crowds that gathered at every stop along his route.

At Fort Worth, Texas, for example, he flew a series of figure-eights between two water towers only forty feet apart. His plane had a wingspread of 32 feet, so Rodgers was really playing the daredevil that day. Outside Waco, Texas, a giant eagle started to follow the *Vin-Fiz Flyer*. Rodgers turned sharply, then dived to frighten the eagle away. If bird had attacked plane, who knows what damage might have been done?

Despite engine breakdowns, Rodgers flew across New Mexico and reached Tucson, Arizona, by November 1. The next day he set out for California. By this time he was asking for more than his plane had to give. Over the desert a cylinder exploded. Hot oil covered Rodgers's face and goggled eyes, and countless steel splinters drove themselves into his right arm. He managed to guide his plane down safely.

Rodgers spent the next two days in bed while his repair crew patched up the engine again. In the air once more, he was flying through San Gorgona Pass when the same old engine troubles, and more, erupted. The oil tank leaked oil; the radiator leaked water; the magneto plugs worked their way out of the sockets; a connecting rod broke. Rodgers's right arm ached badly; his head ached, too. But he made it in one piece to an alfalfa field outside Banning, California.

On November 5 Rodgers flew the 67 miles from Banning to Pasadena, California. There a cheering crowd carried him, cold cigar in his mouth, to the official welcoming committee awaiting him. Some people offered their sympathies over the lost Hearst prize. "The money isn't everything," he said. "I made it, didn't I?"

Rodgers was the first to fly from coast to coast. In all, his trip had taken forty-nine days, but he had actually been in the air only 103 hours. He had covered the distance at an average speed of nearly 52 miles an hour. Of the original *Vin-Fiz Flyer* in which he had left New York, only the vertical rudder and the drip pan had lasted the entire flight. Everything else, including the engine, had been replaced or completely rebuilt at least once.

Rodgers stayed in California to enjoy his triumph and to plan new daredevil feats. On April 3, 1912, he was stunt-flying low over a San Diego beach, lifting his hands from the controls in a foolish show of defiant bravery. His plane plunged into the shallow water. The engine crushed Rodgers to death.

The name of Calbraith Perry Rodgers has been largely forgotten now. But in his time he was both daredevil and hero of the new science, the new art, the new sport of aviation.

Daredevil No. 2

LINCOLN BEACHEY, though he also is forgotten now, was another daredevil whose name and fame were trumpeted loudly in his time. He started his air career at the age of seventeen by piloting Captain Thomas Baldwin's airship around St. Louis, Missouri in 1904. Two years later he was the first airship pilot to fly around the Washington Monument in the national capital. His airship in those days consisted of a gas bag from which hung a treadway. He walked up and down the treadway to control the *Rubber Cow*, the apt name of the craft.

In 1910 Beachey enrolled in the Curtiss flying school at Hammondsport, New York. At first his airship experience seemed to count for nothing—he was a poor, even suicide-prone, student. Almost every landing ended in a crash. Eventually Beachey caught on and became the leading flier of the Curtiss exhibition team.

One of Beachey's stunts was to repeat his flight around the Washington Monument, this time in a biplane. Another was to fly low over Niagara Falls, going under the suspension bridge and almost skimming the torrent. Beachey's real contribution to early aviation, however, was to figure out a way to come safely out of a spin.

In those days going into a spin was a deadly hazard for pilots. A spinning plane nearly always crashed because the pilot tried to fight the spin by kicking his rudder against it. Beachey saw that auto drivers saved themselves when skidding on ice by steering in the skid's direction, not against it. Eventually the skid loses its power and the driver regains control. Beachey applied that thinking to an airplane spin. He kept his rudder with the spin and soon saw the spin weaken. The craft leveled off and was out of danger.

Beachey preached his skid-control gospel and other safety measures to all of his stunt-flier friends. Despite his own daredevil feats, he was a missionary for air safety. He actually dropped out of stunt flying for a time because many pilots who tried to imitate his stunts were crashing to their deaths.

On March 15, 1915, Beachey, age twenty-eight, crashed to his own death. At the San Francisco Exhibition he was flying a plane of his own design, the *Lincoln Beachey Special*. One of his old stunts was the "death dive," in which he would dive straight down from a considerable altitude and level off only at the last moment. This time he did not pull out. His plane plunged into the deep waters of San Francisco Bay.

CHAPTER 3
A DUTCH DESIGNER AND A GERMAN ACE OF ACES
ANTHONY FOKKER, MANFRED VON RICHTHOFEN (THE RED BARON)

"When my brother and I built and flew the first man-carrying flying machine, we thought we were introducing into the world an invention which would make further wars practically impossible."

A saddened Orville Wright wrote that in 1917. World War I, which raged between 1914 and 1918, showed Wright how vain his earlier hope had been. Instead of abolishing war, the airplane made the wars of the twentieth century only more devastating and destructive. Military aircraft have grown from the slow and clumsy observation planes of 1914 to today's sleek supersonic jets. Now vast fleets of fighters and bombers make up the first line of offense and defense for nearly every major nation in the world.

The start of World War I came suddenly on June 28, 1914. On that day the Archduke Francis Ferdinand of Austria-Hungary was assassinated at Sarajevo, capital of the Austrian province of Bosnia. His killer, Gavrilo Princip, was a Serb. The slaying was an excuse to set off a war that had long been simmering between Austria-Hungary and Serbia.

Soon much of the rest of Europe was drawn into the conflict. Germany, which had been itching for a war, joined its political partner, Austria-Hungary. Turkey and Bulgaria jumped in, too, and the four became known as the Central Powers. Opposing them were Britain, France, Russia, Italy, and other nations, soon to be known as the Allies. (The United States did not enter the war until 1917, about a year and a half before it ended.)

By August 1914 a full-scale war was about to begin. The airplane had been in existence for less than eleven years, yet it already figured in the plans of the generals. Aircraft had first been used in fighting in 1911, when Mexican government planes scouted rebel camps from the air, counting men and weapons. That same year the Italians had flown over their Turkish foes and dropped bombs. In 1912 participants in the Balkan War had spied on one another from the skies.

At the start of World War I the Germans were said to have about 1,200 military planes on hand. The British and French may have had a combined total of about a thousand. But these figures are misleading. Only a few of these planes were ready to fly, and the number of trained pilots on either side was small. Thus each of the major countries at war was frantically scrambling to teach more pilots and get more planes into the air.

Meet Tony Fokker

THE NETHERLANDS (Holland) was geographically well within the boundaries of the fighting. Still it managed to remain neutral through the whole of World War I. Despite his country's neutrality, a young Dutchman named Anthony Fokker helped keep German planes flying almost to the end of World War I.

Fokker, only twenty-four when the war started, was no crack flier himself. Instead he was a designer of new planes (not above stealing the ideas of others), an industrialist who set up many aircraft factories, and an inventor who prided himself on being a good businessman.

Tony Fokker's father was a rich tea planter who had moved his family back to the Netherlands from Java in the East Indies when the boy was six. Tony did poorly at school; his mind was on experiments and inventions, not on arithmetic and spelling. He built himself a toy electric train and tried to tap an outside power line to run it. He did tap a gas main for his gas-combustion engine and almost set the house ablaze.

Early on, young Fokker became fascinated by airplanes. He built paper and wooden models, altering the Wrights' basic design. Avoiding compulsory army service, he attended engineering schools in Germany for a time. Then he built his own plane and flew it over the birthday party in Amsterdam for Holland's Queen Wilhelmina.

In 1912 Fokker joined a group at the Johannesthal airfield near Berlin. Assembled here were young pilots trying out planes of their own design or testing the aircraft of other builders. Fokker soon became the leading pilot at the field. Then he went into aircraft manufacturing. Soon there was more and more talk of war, and Germany was busily preparing for it.

Fokker got a flood of orders from the German army and navy, and the money began rolling in. For a time he thought of retiring with his new wealth, but he was already too deeply involved. When the war actually started, Fokker's factories were turning out scores of new aircraft. Fokker was testing, demonstrating, and redesigning his planes as well as supervising their construction.

The early World War I planes were not fighters or bombers. They were two-seater observation craft: the pilot flew the plane, and the observer took aerial photos of the enemy's troops and big guns. The observer also spotted the results of artillery fire from his own forces. Often he carried a rifle, just in case an enemy plane came close enough for him to take a shot at it.

Soon the air above the front lines became thick with observation planes from both sides. They began shooting at each other in earnest. But those early two-seaters were awkward to fly, and it was hard to swing an observer into position so that he could fire his rifle. Nor could a pilot easily evade an enemy observer finally in position to shoot at him. So within several months the two-seaters began to

Anthony Fokker, second from left, points out aircraft feature to friends at his post-World War I airplane factory in New Jersey.

give way to the more maneuverable single-seaters. The observer was eliminated, and the pilot was armed with a machine gun.

Right away the use of a machine gun presented problems. When firing straight forward, which was most of the time, the pilot had to shoot through the swiftly whirling blades of the propeller. Nothing but chance prevented the bullets from hitting the prop. The problem was turned over to Tony Fokker, who swiftly solved it. He timed the gun with the plane engine so that the shots avoided the propeller rotation.

When asked to demonstrate this "interrupter gear" in actual combat, Fokker went aloft in one of his own planes. He got within firing range of a French Farman aircraft, then would not pull the trigger. He decided that "the whole job could go to hell.. . .I had no wish to kill Frenchmen for Germans. Let them do their own killing."

The Red Baron

TONY FOKKER kept on producing planes all through the war. One German pilot admired his aircraft and used them in preference to all other German makes. His name is remembered perhaps above all other World War I fliers.

Today the Red Baron appears regularly in the Charles Schulz comic strip, *Peanuts*. The baron is a comic figure in the Lufthansa airline ads and commercials. His memory is evoked in a semi-serious cult that commands thousands of followers. In real life he was Baron Manfred von Richthofen.

Richthofen was the German "ace of aces" in World War I. Fighting furiously in air battles over the Western Front, he shot down eighty Allied planes. What kind of a man was this young Red Baron? What drove him so relentlessly month after month as he chalked up kill after kill? What did he contribute to the art and science of flight?

Looking at his family and his boyhood gives us an answer to the first question. His father was a retired army officer; his mother came from an aristocratic home. Manfred, their first child, was born in 1892. Two more boys, Lothar and Bolko, and a girl, Ilse, followed. The family lived on a wooded estate near Schweidnitz, in Silesia.

Young Manfred hunted often. On horseback, his gun in the crook of his arm, his dogs ranging ahead, the boy enjoyed being alone in the woods. Being by himself was Manfred's way of rebelling against the pressures put on him to study, to behave, to conform.

At eleven, Manfred entered the Cadet Corps, a junior military school for boys who looked forward to army careers. In class he worked just hard enough to scrape through, but in the gym and on the playground he was a demon. He was skilled at gymnastics, especially on the horizontal bar.

And he seemed to love taking chances, taking risks. One time he shinnied up the lightning-rod mount to the tall steeple of his school. At the very top he tied his handkerchief. Ten years later he visited his younger brother Bolko at the school. The handkerchief was still there.

Came Easter 1911, and Richthofen's cadet days were over. He entered the German army and was assigned to a cavalry regiment. The next year he was commissioned *leutnant* (lieutenant). Later he wrote, "I had a colossal liking for serving with my regiment. It is the finest thing for a young soldier to be a cavalryman."

Richthofen was on the Russian front when World War I broke out. Soon his regiment was transferred to Belgium.

Richthofen was restless because he and his men, their horses taken away, were put in rear-line trenches. He could hear the roar of the big guns, but he could see only mud and barbed wire.

The airplanes Richthofen saw overhead promised to give him the action he wanted. He asked for a transfer and got it. After four weeks of training, he qualified as an aerial observer.

Back on the Russian front, Richthofen was teamed with a daredevil sportsman, Count Holck. Their last flight together nearly ended in disaster. They had been flying low over a burning Russian village to assess the damage. Suddenly a thick column of smoke trapped the plane and sent it spinning down. Holck was barely able to pull out of the spin and away from the smoke before the engine conked out.

"We went lower and lower [recorded Richthofen] and just managed to glide over a forest and land at an abandoned artillery position. I told Holck that the evening before I had reported that this very site was still being held by the Russians. We jumped from the plane and ran for the woods for cover. All I had was a pistol and six cartridges. Holck had nothing.

"When we reached the woods I turned, and with my glasses watched a soldier run toward our plane. I got a chill when I saw he wore a cap instead of a spiked helmet. I was certain he was a Russian, but when the man came near, Holck shouted for joy. He recognized the man as a grenadier of the Prussian Guards. They had stormed this position at daybreak."

Sensing that observers were soon to be eliminated, Richthofen began taking flying lessons. He wanted to pilot one of the new fighter planes just coming into use. As a young cadet, Richthofen had been a poor student. He was an equally poor student pilot. He took twenty-five lessons before he was permitted to solo. And on this first solo flight he lost control of his plane and crash-landed. This did not disturb him. He picked himself up and began flying again. By Christmas 1915 he was a qualified pilot.

After more service on the Russian front, Richthofen came back to the Somme River region in northern France. Here the British and French held control of the sky. The Allied airmen bombed German supply depots, photographed troop movements, and directed artillery fire. Germany was determined to drive the Allies from the Somme valley.

For nineteen months Richthofen went up almost daily, weather permitting, from his Somme air base to wage aerial war against the enemy. If he once had had any notion that war was an adventure, a game, he soon abandoned it. For him war was now grim and ugly, to be finished as quickly as possible.

Nor did he ever think about the larger questions: was war itself wrong, was the killing it brought ever justified? All he knew was that Germany was involved in a struggle to the death and that he, as a patriotic German, must do his part.

And as a fighter pilot and squadron commander, Richthofen did his part well. Judged only on the number of enemy planes shot down, eighty in all, he did better than any other pilot on either side during World War I. Among his medals was the coveted Pour le Mérite award, better known as the Blue Max. (The award was begun—and given its French name—by Frederick the Great, who loved all things French.)

Richthofen's orders to his squadron were crisp, short,

logical. Even in battle he was terrifyingly calm: "In such a position one thinks calmly and collectedly and weighs the probability of hitting and being hit. As a rule, the fight itself is the least exciting part of the business. If you get excited in air fighting you are sure to make mistakes; you will never get the enemy down. Besides, calmness is a matter of habit."

One time, when Richthofen had ten enemy planes to his credit, he nearly met his match. Flying an Albatros, he encountered the British ace Major Lanoe Hawker in the sky over the German-held part of the Somme. Hawker, in a De Havilland, had downed nine German planes.

For more than half an hour the two circled each other, each trying to get the other in his gun sights. Then Hawker saw that his fuel was running low and attempted a dash to his own lines. Richthofen was not trying for a kill; he wanted only to force Hawker to land and be taken prisoner.

But Hawker was too slippery; he seemed about to make it to safety. Richthofen had to fire directly on Hawker himself. His Spandau guns spit out their shells,

Manfred von Richthofen, the Red Baron, in a formal photo. Pour le Mérite ("Blue Max") award is pinned to his turtleneck.

killing the Englishman instantly. The flaming De Havilland crashed into an abandoned building.

By July 6, 1917, Richthofen had scored fifty-seven air victories. That day he was engaged in raging combat with a group of British Sopwiths. Coming in close, he was struck by a bullet that scraped his skull. He fought to keep his senses as he landed his plane behind his own lines. Later he remembered, "At that moment the idea struck me: *This is how it feels when one is shot down to his death.*"

In the operating room, doctors found that the bullet had exposed the skull but had not penetrated it. Richthofen had missed death by a fraction of an inch. He was back with his squadron only nineteen days later, but he had not really recovered. He was in and out of the hospital several times during the following weeks. When he first went aloft again, he was sick and shaky. But he managed to send another British plane down in flames.

After he shot down his sixtieth airplane, Richthofen went home on leave. He tried to relax, but that proved impossible. He worried about his brother Lothar, now a member of his squadron. He worried even more about the outcome of the war. He told his mother that Germany was going to be defeated.

On April 21, 1918, British and Australian troops were entrenched on one side of the Somme. Facing them were German infantry regiments, with German airfields not far behind. Soon after dawn, Richthofen's squadron was in the air, probing for weaknesses in the Allied defenses. Richthofen was flying a Fokker triplane painted bright red except for the black and white German cross on each side of the fuselage.

Rising to meet Richthofen was a group of British fighters in Sopwith Camels. In command was Captain

Arthur Roy Brown, a Canadian pilot. Newest in the group was Lieutenant Wilfred May, who had never flown in combat before. Brown's instructions to May had been explicit: "Stay on the outskirts of the fighting. Watch and learn. If you by any chance manage to bag an enemy plane, streak for the base. You'll have done enough for one day."

But May could not hold back. He blundered into the thick of the blazing tangle and sent one Fokker limping for home. Then he tried to fight his way free, only to find the Red Baron himself on his tail—and closing in fast.

Roy Brown spotted the chase and joined in. Richthofen soon realized that he was being tracked down, and he tried to maneuver his way out. Brown got close enough to fire a volley before he veered away.

By now Richthofen was only a few hundred feet above the ground. He flew directly over an Australian machine-gun emplacement. The Australians, expert gunners all, fired away at the plane almost overhead. Soon the red Fokker made a forced landing inside the Australian lines.

When the Australian soldiers approached the Fokker they found the pilot dead, a bullet through his heart. His papers identified him: Baron Manfred von Richthofen, Germany's greatest fighter pilot, the most feared airman of them all. The Australians and the British buried him with full military honors.

Who had shot Richthofen down—Captain Roy Brown or the Aussie gunners? Armchair experts debated this question for years. It was finally settled to most people's satisfaction by Dale Fitler in his book, *The Day the Red Baron Died* (see Bibliography). Here Fitler shows that the credit properly belongs to the Australians.

CHAPTER
TWO BRITISH ACES

ALBERT BALL, BILLY BISHOP

When World War I started, Britain's air arm was made up of two separate services: the Royal Flying Corps and the Royal Naval Air Service. It was not until 1918 that the two combined as the Royal Air Force.

The first British officer to fly was Captain Bertram Dickson. Winning his wings in 1911, Dickson predicted that in the war soon to break out, "both sides would be equipped with large corps of aeroplanes, each trying to obtain information of the other."

But the airplane crew would soon do far more than just observe, he predicted: "The efforts which each would exert in order to hinder or prevent the enemy from obtaining information" would lead to a struggle for control of the air by fighter pilots.

At the war's start, Britain could send only forty-eight planes across the English Channel to help the French against the swiftly advancing German forces. At Dover, England, on the channel coast, the planes were loaded with provisions as if for an expedition—canned beef, chocolate bars, bottles of water, small cooking stoves, and auto-tire inner tubes to serve as life preservers.

The forty-eight planes made it across the channel without mishap and settled at an airfield near Maubeuge, France. The pilots began daily observation flights, but soon found that the French ground troops were firing at every plane they saw, friend or enemy. And when the first British troops joined the French, the British pilots were horrified to realize that their own countrymen, like the French, were shooting at every plane in sight.

Gradually, however, the ground troops learned to tell friend from foe. Soon more British fliers joined their comrades-at-arms in France. They were stationed at airfields all over the northern part of the country, and they went aloft, sometimes three times a day, looking for trouble. At first their only duty was to look around and snap photos, or perhaps drop a homemade bomb or two that caused little damage. In time they became fighter pilots, engaging the enemy in air duels that often ended in victory for one and death for the other.

As were the fliers of the other warring nations, the British pilots were young—most in their late teens or early twenties. At the height of the war, casualties (deaths or injuries) were numerous. In fact, many pilots were at the front for just weeks before they were shot down.

To compensate for the death or the years in a prisoner-of-war camp that awaited them, the British fliers managed to live the good life when they were on the ground. They had orderlies (batmen) who served as valets and cooks. Their quarters were comfortable, the food was good, and French wines were plentiful. Whenever they could, they went off to Paris for a few days to enjoy the pleasures of that still gay capital city. But they could not ignore the deaths of their friends or the good possibility of their own destruction on their very next flight.

The British public was eager to hear of their pilots' brave doings. The British government, aided by the press, focused attention on a few pilots and made them air heroes. No doubt they earned their praise. No doubt, too, there were many others who deserved the same publicity but did not get it.

Albert Ball, Early British Ace

THE FIRST British pilot to win national acclaim was Albert Ball, the son of a country estate manager. His early passion was for engines and radios, tinkering with them and picking up Morse code messages from all over Europe. He had another passion—for the violin—that later made it hard for him to accept the slaughter of war.

As a teenager Ball went into business for himself as an engineer and operator of a brass foundry. War soon came along, and Ball volunteered. Right away he decided that flying was for him. In his spare time he began taking flying lessons at a civilian flying school near his army base. When he got his pilot's papers he requested duty with the Royal Flying Corps (RFC).

It took some time to learn how to fly the RFC way. After a while he got the hang of it and was sent to France to fly B.E. 2c observation planes. It was early in 1916, and Ball was only nineteen years old.

Ball's first squadron worked with British ground

48/ *ACES, HEROES, AND DAREDEVILS OF THE AIR*

troops. It photographed German trenches, spotted British artillery fire, and dropped some bombs. That was dangerous duty. The B.E. 2c's were raked by German antiaircraft guns and attacked by Fokker fighters. The British were suffering heavy losses.

Youthful Captain Albert Ball, British ace, stands before plane. Ball loved music and flowers, but he was ruthless as a destroyer of the enemy.

The danger did not disturb Ball. Several times he swung his B.E. 2c into position so that his observer could fire back at the Fokkers. When Ball wasn't flying his B.E. 2c, he was up in a single-seated Bristol Scout learning how to control the plane and fire its Lewis machine gun at the same time.

In time Ball was transferred to a fighter squadron equipped with Nieuport Scouts. At once he began racking up a notable score against the Germans. Included in his record were a number of hits against tethered balloons sent up by the enemy to observe artillery results. These balloons and the observers they carried were a real help to their own big guns—and a real danger to the other side.

Ball used several tricks to lure enemy pilots to their doom. One was to let the foe get on his tail. Then, at the moment the enemy was about to start blazing away with his Spandau guns, Ball would slam his rudder into a tight turn and come up on the German's tail. Another trick was to go for the enemy head on, in a collision course. Ball counted on the foe losing his nerve before he did. When the German veered away, Ball opened fire.

In late 1916 Ball was posted to a training group, where he was supposed to teach new pilots. He didn't like the duty and plagued his senior officers to be allowed to return to the front.

At the same time he wrote his mother: "I am, indeed, looked after by God; but oh, I do get tired of always living to kill." It was a sentiment he shared with many others—the feeling that he must go on with a job he hated in order to get it over as soon as possible.

By February 1917 Ball was again on the fighting line, this time as flight commander with another squadron. Before, Ball had usually gone up by himself, seeking out an enemy and destroying him without help. Now he was the leader of a group of six pilots who counted on him. The squadron flew twice a day, but Ball still found time to venture forth alone.

On one of these solo flights Ball engaged two enemy aircraft, firing at them until his ammunition was gone. The Germans headed for home, with Ball following close behind. As they landed, Ball dropped them a note saying in effect, "Meet me here tomorrow, same time," signed with his name. That name was already well known to the Germans; they were eager to bring him down.

The next day Ball found two German planes circling in the sky, waiting for him. He attacked at once, only to find three more German aircraft on his tail. No matter; Ball was ready to take on all comers. For several minutes the six planes were locked in furious struggle. Ball was holding his own until his ammunition ran out. Running away was impossible. What to do?

Ball saw a large field directly below. He glided to a landing, and as his plane stopped, he lay back in his seat faking a serious injury. Three of the Germans streaked for home. Were they ready to broadcast the news that the famous British ace Albert Ball had been brought down?

The other two planes landed nearby, and their pilots came running toward Ball. As soon as they were away from their aircraft, Ball gunned his own engine and took off into the blue. The Germans were left standing, confused and confounded by Ball's trick.

Ball's squadron had fought against Richthofen's unit several times, but Ball and the German ace had never met in direct combat. In May 1917 word got back to the British that the Red Baron was home on extended leave and that his brother Lothar was now in command of the squadron. This was the time, the British planners decided, to meet the Richthofen fliers in a fight. Two squadrons, one of them Ball's, were chosen for the mission.

On May 7 the two British teams flew over the German-held airfield at Douai, France. The Richthofen fighters rose to meet them. The sky was thick with planes, like angry bees buzzing furiously at one another. Then, suddenly, it began to rain hard. The British attack became disorganized. Ball flew to a nearby rendezvous. There he joined two other members of his squadron and set out to seek further combat.

Ball spotted a red Fokker and followed it into an enveloping cloud. He never made it out of the cloud alive. A German machine-gun crew, perched on a church steeple, shot him down. Ball, who had destroyed forty-three enemy aircraft, was twenty years old when he died.

Billy Bishop Goes to War

ANOTHER YOUNG hero who flew for the British destroyed seventy-two German planes and lived to describe his exploits to his grandchildren. William Bishop was a Canadian who served in the Royal Flying Corps and the Royal Air Force. Many people regard Bishop as the greatest Allied fighter pilot in World War I, perhaps equal to Richthofen himself.

Consider the honors heaped on Bishop. He achieved the rank of lieutenant colonel. He was awarded the Victoria Cross, Distinguished Service Order and Bar, Military Cross, Distinguished Flying Cross, Legion of Honor, and

Croix de Guerre with palm. In World War II he was appointed air marshal, an honorary post in the Royal Canadian Air Force, and served in Canada's recruitment drive. And in 1980 his adventures were made into *Billy Bishop Goes to War*, a musical play that earned good reviews in Washington, D. C., and New York.

Bishop was born in Owen Sound, a small town in the hills of Ontario, Canada. He was an outdoor boy, not good in school but keen on sports and hunting. At the age of twelve he entered Owen Sound Collegiate, a prep school for the Royal Military College at Kingston, in which he was enrolled at seventeen. He was twenty when the war started in Europe.

At once he joined the Mississauga Horse, a Canadian cavalry regiment, because it was soon to sail for England. But the Mississauga Horse lingered overlong in training in the muddy English countryside. Billy Bishop grew impatient and looked to the skies. He saw British aircraft flying overhead and knew that they were on their way to see action. "That's for me," Bishop decided.

Transferring to the RFC, he qualified as an observer after some training and was sent to France. His first job was to go up with a pilot in an old two-seater and guide the firing of the British big guns. He wanted desperately to fly his own plane, and after several months he got his wish—the hard way.

The plane on which Bishop was serving as observer struck something hard on landing, and Bishop's knee was badly injured. He was sent back to England to recover. Months later, knee back in shape, he was accepted for pilot training. He got his wings and was first posted to a unit flying in defense of London against the raiding German zeppelins.

These huge dirigibles, based in Friedrichshafen, Germany, flew over London and dropped bombs from altitudes as great as 20,000 feet. The bomb damage was heavy; so was the fear in the hearts of many Londoners. But Bishop's plane was old, incapable of climbing anywhere near the heights reached by the zeppelins. Bishop was eager to see real action, preferably in France and in his own fast single-seat fighter.

At last in March 1917 he was sent to France to join No. 60 Squadron. He was assigned a new Nieuport fighter. On his first real flight he was given the job of escorting bomber planes in an attack on retreating German ground troops. On the way the formation was pounced upon by three Albatros fighters. Bishop got one of them in his sights and followed the plane down to 2,000 feet, firing all the way. To his satisfaction he saw the Albatros go into a spin and crash into the ground. It was Bishop's first air victory.

Bishop himself was soon in trouble—engine trouble. He managed to glide his plane to earth just inside his own lines and hide it from enemy artillery fire. When it was dark and safe enough to come out of hiding, he found the trouble: oily plugs. Bishop cleaned these with a handy toothbrush. At dawn he was on his way home.

Captain Albert Ball was also attached to No. 60 Squadron. Ball was a strange figure who played classical music on his wind-up phonograph and kept his room filled with cut flowers. He was also the leading ace of all the Allied pilots at the time.

It was Ball who took Billy Bishop as a friend and taught him some tricks of his death-dealing trade. One of these was, when greatly outnumbered, to stick close to the tail of an enemy plane. The others would hold their fire for fear of hitting one of their own. Ball would watch to see if one of the German planes chose to separate itself from the group. When it did so, Ball would open fire on the one he was tailing, then spin off to attack the one who broke away. This would throw the enemy into confusion, and Ball would streak back to his base.

Under Ball's teaching, Bishop's score mounted. During six weeks in April and May 1917 he destroyed twenty German planes. Like Ball, he did his most savage killing when flying alone. Later he wrote: "I had become very ambitious, and was hoping to get a large number of [enemy planes] officially credited to me.... With this object in view I planned many little expeditions of my own, and with the use of great patience, I was very successful in one or two."

On June 2, 1917, he was off on one of those "little expeditions." His self-designed mission was to sneak up on an unsuspecting enemy airfield and destroy its aircraft on the ground or as they rose to meet him. He found such a field near Cambrai, France. Speeding across it at an altitude of only fifty feet, he fired at the planes on the ground. He demolished one, then another, as they were taking off. Two more were already in the air, ready to fight. He destroyed one of them, but the other broke away.

Now Bishop was out of ammunition and ready to return to his base. But other planes were in swift pursuit of him. He shook them off and made it back to safety. On landing he looked over his Nieuport. More than a hundred shells had pierced its wings and fuselage. Pilot and engine had been miraculously spared.

Despite his daredevil reputation, Bishop was actually a cautious flier. No pilot defies caution and lives for very long. One time, however, Bishop forgot—and was very nearly killed because of his forgetfulness.

He was flying over Armentières, France, when he spotted a lone Albatros. He closed in for the kill. If he had looked behind him, as he should have, he would have seen five more Albatroses on his tail. He destroyed the first one, and only then realized the danger he was in.

Bishop wheeled to meet his pursuers head on. One of them veered away too sharply and crash-landed. Bishop followed a second, but his own guns jammed and one of his ailerons was damaged. The German plane was in worse shape. Its wing fabric was torn and many of its struts (wing supports) were broken. Bishop maneuvered his plane until his wing was under that of the Albatros. Then he turned into the enemy with a screaming crash. He then managed to wiggle his own plane free and stay in the air, watching the Albatros fall to earth.

After he was made leader of No. 85 Squadron, Bishop's tally rose to forty-seven. By June 1918 his commanders decided he had done enough. In two weeks he was to return to England. In those two weeks Bishop destroyed another twenty-five German planes. He flew and fought like a demon.

On his last day Bishop took on three Pfalz fighters and shot down one of them. Two more Pfalz planes joined in the ruckus. All four circled, waiting for one to lead the attack. Finally two flew at Bishop. At once he dived between them, and the two ran into each other and crashed. The other two fled, and Bishop got one with his Lewis guns. The last one escaped, to Bishop's disappointment.

Bishop died in 1956, one of the few top-ranking Allied pilots in World War I to die peacefully in his bed in his advancing years.

CHAPTER 5
THREE FRENCH FLIERS

ROLAND GARROS, GEORGES GUYNEMER,
RENÉ FONCK

When the "guns of August" 1914 were first fired, France had a total of 138 planes ready for combat. The count comprised eleven different models, all named for their manufacturers—the two-seater Voisins, Farmans, Bregeuts (all biplanes with their engines in the rear) and the front-engine Bleriot and Morane-Saulnier monoplanes, to name only a few.

At first the pilots were mainly enlisted men, who were treated like chauffeurs or cabdrivers. The observers were the real bosses. Because there was no mechanical or electronic way for pilot and observer to communicate with each other aloft, they had to scream into the wind or pass notes.

On October 5, 1914, the French chalked up a first in military aviation history. That day Corporal Louis Quenault was in the observer's front seat of a Voisin piloted by

Sergeant Joseph Frantz. Fitted to Quenault's cockpit was a Hotchkiss machine gun. The two were on an observation flight—and ready for trouble.

Over Rheims, France, they sighted a German Aviatik. Swinging his Voisin into position, Frantz closed in. The German was not expecting an armed foe in the air. He was surely astonished when Quenault opened fire with his Hotchkiss. The Aviatik went down all ablaze. It earned the dubious distinction of being the first plane to be shot down from the air by a machine gun.

The Voisin the Frenchmen were flying was a pusher plane, its engine and propeller in the rear. The propeller presented no obstacle to the observer, who fired his machine gun from the forward cockpit. But the pusher planes proved slow and clumsy and were gradually replaced by planes with propellers in the front.

Garros Finds an Answer

IMMEDIATELY THE plane designers were faced with a problem: how to fire a machine gun through the swiftly turning propeller blades. Tony Fokker found the answer, as we have seen, for the Germans. But months before Fokker perfected his interrupter gear, a French airman named Roland Garros found a different solution. It gave the French an early advantage in their air battles with the Germans.

Garros was born on the island of Réunion, a French possession in the Indian Ocean. His father, a wealthy lawyer, saw that young Roland had talent. He could draw, paint, play the piano. At twenty he was sent to Paris to study for the concert stage.

Instead of entering a music conservatory, Garros met

Albert Santos-Dumont, noted air pioneer. Garros at once plunked down his tuition money for flying lessons with Santos-Dumont. Within months Garros was winning flying prizes all over Europe. Just before the war started he was in Germany giving flight shows and lectures, using his own Morane monoplane for demonstrations.

Then the announcement of the war's start was flashed across the world. Garros, a young man of twenty-six, was in a panic. Here he was, still in Germany, and the French authorities well knew that he had been promoting the commercial and military uses of aviation before crowds of enthusiastic Germans. If he stayed in Germany he might be locked up. If he made it back to France he might be jailed there as well. He decided to take his chances with the French.

Garros packed his bags, sneaked out of his hotel, and found his way to the hangar where his Morane was parked. He opened the hangar door, swiftly revved up his engine, and escaped into the evening darkness. Few pilots had ever before flown at night, but Garros found his way to the Swiss border and landed safely. In a few days he was in Paris signing up for military service.

Soon in the air, Garros at once began trying to solve the problem of shooting through the propeller blades without hitting them. He found a fairly simple solution: metal deflector plates bolted to the propeller blades. In experiments he fired round after round of machine-gun bullets with no damage to the props. The method worked—and Garros was ready to try out his solution in combat.

The test came on April 1, 1915. Garros took off alone on a mission to bomb a railroad station at Ostend, Belgium. On the way he encountered an Albatros. Garros went straight at the enemy, blazing away with his machine gun, the bullets shooting their way through the whirling propeller. The German plane had no chance. It went down with a crash.

Two weeks later Garros downed a second German plane and on April 18 a third. In a second flight on that same day Garros was himself shot down behind enemy lines. Unhurt, he crawled out of his wrecked Morane and tried to set fire to it. He wanted to conceal the deflector plates on his propeller.

It was a damp day, and nothing would burn, not even the hay that Garros stuffed into the cockpit to act as tinder. He tried to run away but was soon caught. His plane was found and his invention taken for study.

Garros spent the next thirty-three months in a prisoner-of-war camp. He escaped at last and rejoined the French air force. A month before the war was over in 1918 he was shot down and killed by a German flying a new model of a Fokker.

Guynemer Battles Illness, German Foe

THE GARROS story properly belongs in the early history of French wartime aviation. The Guynemer story spans the first three of the four years of World War I. Georges Guynemer was one of the greatest fighter pilots of that savage conflict.

The father of Georges Marie Ludovic Jules Guynemer had been an army officer, but the boy didn't seem likely to take up his father's career. Georges was a sick, skinny child, overprotected by his mother and sisters. He was a good student, however, and a good mechanic.

When war came in 1914 young Guynemer tried to join

the army, but was rejected several times for medical reasons. His father used his influence, and the youth was finally allowed to enlist as a student mechanic in the French air arm. He spent the first several months cleaning aircraft engines and sweeping out hangars. Then his father applied pressure again, and Guynemer was taken into the pilot training program.

Guynemer was still sickly and underweight, but he had good vision, hearing, and coordination. He turned out to be an exceptionally able pilot. Guynemer spent countless hours practicing landings and takeoffs. And for more hours he sat in the pilot's seat when the plane was on the ground, rehearsing his use of the instruments.

He always won complete mastery of whatever plane he was flying. As one of his biographers, Robert Jackson, says in *Fighter Pilots of World War I* (see Bibliography): "He nursed his aircraft lovingly and was completely at one with it; he knew every sound, every vibration it made, just as though his machine was a sentient thing with a personality of its own."

Guynemer won his first aerial duel on July 19, 1915. He was flying a Morane, with Lieutenant Guerder as his observer, when they met a German Aviatik inside the French lines. Guynemer put his plane below and to the left of the Aviatik. He opened fire and saw that his salvo wounded his foe. The German, armed only with a rifle, fired back and hit Guerder.

Then the Aviatik spun into a flaming crash. Guynemer, wanting medical attention for the wounded Guerder, tried to land but was hit by enemy ground fire. Coasting into a haystack, he broke his propeller.

The war had been going on for nearly a year, and the

French public was hungry for news of French military victories. Such successes had been in short supply. The French press lavishly praised Guynemer and Guerder, and both were awarded the Medaille Militaire. For Guynemer it was the first of fifty-four victories.

Guynemer went on scoring hits until March 1916, when he very nearly lost his life. His squadron had been sent to Verdun to help French infantry and artillery defend that massive fortified line against a powerful German attack. On the day he reached Verdun, Guynemer tangled with three Fokkers. He was wounded twice in the left arm, and shell fragments cut into his cheek and eyelids. Finally eluding his pursuers, he landed safely. French medics hauled him from his Nieuport, bloody but unwilling to give up.

Sent to a Paris hospital, Guynemer rebelled against his confinement. In a few weeks, his wounds only half healed, he walked out of the hospital and rejoined his unit. His chief ordered him back at once for further medical treatment. When he was finally released from the hospital, Guynemer resumed flying. By September 1916 he had recorded eighteen victories, making him the leading French ace.

In the fall of 1916 Guynemer was flying the new Spad, a French fighter with a 150-horsepower Hispano-Suiza engine. During eighteen days in November he shot down four Albatroses, two LVG's, and one Fokker. By the time he reached his twenty-second birthday his score was twenty-five, and he had been awarded more medals than any other French pilot.

Guynemer's opponents had forced him down at least eight times, but he always made his way home with only minor wounds. His unit, now known as the Escadrille des Cigognes, the Storks Squadron, was the most famous in France, thanks largely to Guynemer's aerial exploits.

But by summer of 1917, Guynemer's old physical weaknesses were ready to do what the enemy's shot and shell could not accomplish. He suffered from tuberculosis and deep depression. His kill total was now fifty, but he feared that the lung disease would prevent him from adding to it. To compensate, he drove himself harder and harder, in the air at all hours. He had fainted twice while aloft, but he still would not quit. That summer he downed three more of the "Boche" (French slang for *Germans*).

Guynemer was eager to get going on the morning of September 11, 1917. He had a dread feeling that his days were numbered. He was scheduled to fly a patrol with three other pilots, but only Lieutenant Bozon-Verduraz showed up on time. So the two flew off by themselves and were soon in the thick of a dogfight with several Fokkers.

After two hours Bozon-Verduraz came back alone. He filed this terse report: "At 9:25, together with Captain Guynemer, attacked an enemy two-seater over the lines at Poelcapelle. Made one pass and fired thirty rounds. Captain Guynemer continued to pursue the enemy as I was obliged to break off to avoid eight single-seaters which were preparing to attack me. I did not see Captain Guynemer again...."

Guynemer never returned. Stunned members of the Storks Squadron waited for some hopeful news: that he had fallen behind enemy lines and been taken prisoner; that he had fallen behind his own lines and been hospitalized. No such news was reported. It took a month before the Department of Foreign Affairs in Berlin officially acknowledged his death.

Nor was Guynemer's body ever found. His name became a legend among French fliers, his story told and retold down through the generations.

René Fonck, Ace in Late Disgrace

ALTHOUGH GUYNEMER'S death was not noted officially for a month, German newspapers early credited the kill to Captain Kurt Wisseman. Wisseman did not enjoy his victory for very long. Nineteen days after Guynemer went down, Wisseman was killed by a Frenchman flying a Spad for the Storks Squadron. Guynemer's avenger was René Fonck, who was able to claim seventy-five victories in the air by the end of the war.

Just before the start of World War I, twenty-year-old René Fonck was an engineering student who had taken flight lessons as well. Fonck enlisted early, but was sidetracked into an engineering unit. In the spring of 1915 he won a transfer to the air arm. His civilian flight training served him well, and he was soon aloft as pilot of a Caudron observation plane.

In time Fonck was flying a Caudron equipped with a machine gun. Slow as it was, the Caudron became a potent fighter under Fonck's skilled handling. Fonck scored his first victory with his Caudron. Soon Fonck in his Caudron scored another triumph—without firing a shot. Meeting two German Rumplers in the air, he cut out one of them and sent it fleeing for home. Then he hung grimly onto the tail of the other. No matter how the Rumpler pilot twisted and turned, Fonck was right behind him. Exhausted, the German was forced to land behind French lines.

News of the bloodless victory got around, perhaps

slowly, and Fonck was transferred to the elite Storks Squadron. There he met Georges Guynemer. Five months later he sought out Guynemer's killer and shot him down. But there was no hate in Fonck's heart. It was all part of the deadly game both sides were playing.

During the autumn of 1917 Fonck continued to play that game to win. Bad weather kept him out of the sky for much of the time, but Fonck did not waste his days. He kept himself fit by exercise, and he drank no alcohol at all. He saw what too much liquor was doing to some of his Storks friends, and he wanted none of it.

Fonck worked out a system of inspecting the bullets in his ammunition belts, discarding any with the slightest flaw. In this way he knew his guns would not jam at critical moments. By the end of the year he had destroyed nineteen enemy planes, a score that put him in a third-place tie on the list of living French pilots.

In March 1918 the Storks Squadron was based at Champagne. There they served as part of the massive defense put up by the French to oppose Germany's final big offensive of the war. The French pilots were assigned to fly low over the advancing German troops and gun them down. Fonck later wrote, "We flew so low that we almost touched the enemy's bayonets, watching the compact masses of troops wilt away before our machine guns."

This was a new and different kind of fighting for Fonck and his fellow pilots. In the air a victory meant seeing your single foe go down in a flaming crash. You rarely saw his face; you never regarded him as a human being. It was all so clean and sanitary, like a surgical operation. Now the pilots were engaged in the bloody butchery of men only yards away, seeing them die in agony, their bodies ripped apart.

Bemedaled René Fonck, French "ace of aces" in World War I, lost his good name in World War II because he talked with a high Nazi.

Fonck was sickened by the sight of violent death. Yet it made him only more determined to win the final victory. He became a close student of the art and science of aerial warfare. He inspected downed enemy aircraft for blind spots in the pilot's line of vision. He worked out angles of attack. He kept close tabs on his bullets and used as few as possible in firing on a foe.

All through the spring and summer of 1918 Fonck fought with deadly precision. On one day of devastation

Fonck destroyed six enemy aircraft. As the Armistice (the day the war ended) approached, Fonck's score was pegged at seventy-five, the highest number credited to any Allied pilot and only five short of the Red Baron's record.

After the war Fonck kept on flying. During the 1920s he wanted to be the first to cross the Atlantic in a plane. Using a tri-motor craft furnished him by the Russian-American plane maker, Igor Sikorsky, he tried to take off from New York on September 15, 1926. A fuel tank mishap prevented him from doing so.

Fonck tried again five days later. His undercarriage collapsed and the plane caught fire. Fonck and his copilot escaped, but two crew members died in the blaze. The next year Charles Lindbergh made the crossing alone, and Fonck gave up trying.

In 1920 Fonck helped Hermann Göring, who had commanded the Richthofen unit after the Red Baron died, to get a job as a commercial airline pilot. This simple act of kindness toward a former foe had a bad result. At the start of World War II, twenty years later, Germany had taken over much of France.

Göring was now the No. 2 Nazi, directly under Adolf Hitler. Marshal Pétain, French head of the conquered territory, asked Fonck to talk to Göring. Pétain wanted to know what Hitler was going to do with his conquest.

Fonck saw Göring several times, but nothing came of their talks. When World War II was over, the French put Pétain and others on trial as collaborators. It was then that Fonck's meetings with Göring were remembered.

Fonck was never formally tried, but he was in disgrace, his great achievements in World War I forgotten. He died in 1953, his reputation still in tatters.

CHAPTER 6
A SALUTE TO LAFAYETTE

The United States did not enter World War I until April 1917. Long before that, many Americans were eager to fight on the Allied side against what they considered a brutal and ravaging enemy. They enlisted under the Canadian or the British flag, or in the French Foreign Legion. Many of them transferred to the American armed forces after April 1917.

In 1916, however, the United States was still doggedly neutral. It tried to discourage young and idealistic Americans from volunteering to fight in a war that the U.S. government wanted to keep clear of. Nevertheless, the volunteers slipped across the border into Canada, either enlisting there or taking passage on a ship bound for England or France.

Among these volunteers were many fully qualified civilian pilots—and some who doctored their flight records to indicate they were fully qualified. Those who did not sign on with the Canadians or the British headed straight for Paris.

The Lafayette Escadrille

IN PARIS, the fliers enlisted in what was first called the Escadrille Americaine. The name was changed to the Lafayette Escadrille after the German ambassador in Washington objected to Americans advertising their part in flying for an enemy of Germany. Lafayette, of course, was the young French nobleman, the Marquis de Lafayette, who volunteered to serve under George Washington in the American Revolution. He fought valiantly for the American cause and earned an honored place in American history.

A total of only thirty-eight Americans made up the Lafayette Escadrille. Nearly two hundred other Americans also flew for France in various French squadrons. Despite their separation into these French units, these other Americans were known collectively as the Lafayette Flying Corps.

The Lafayette Escadrille flew for twenty months and managed to down 199 enemy planes. Several Americans became aces under the French, each with five or more planes to his credit. Several others were killed in air battles. But these statistics were not important. What was important was that the Lafayette Escadrille showed the French that America was their friend and that more American aid was on the way.

It was an American named Norman Prince, a pilot from Pride's Crossing, Massachusetts, who got the escadrille idea started. In Paris Prince talked over this idea with other Americans and with the French government. At first the government wanted no part of an all-American unit in its air arm.

But it began to listen to reason when Edmund L. Gros, an American doctor practicing in Paris, added the force of his arguments to those of the Prince group. Dr. Gros had been one of the organizers of the American volunteer ambulance service, and his endorsement carried weight.

The American volunteer fliers were given some combat flight training, then sent to Luxeuil to learn to handle the Nieuport fighters assigned to them. Luxeuil had been a fashionable health spa for hundreds of years, a place where invigorating mineral springs flowed into fancy tubs of pink stone. Flowers and fruit trees covered the landscape, rooms at the inn were comfortable, and food was in the best tradition of French cooking.

The American fliers wore custom-tailored uniforms with Sam Browne belts and swagger sticks. The whole scene resembled a Hollywood movie, except that a very real threat of death awaited the Americans once they engaged the enemy.

In time the escadrille was transferred to the airfield at Bar-le-Duc, near Verdun. One of the Americans, Victor Chapman, wrote to his parents that "this flying is much too romantic to be real modern war with all its horrors." He was soon to learn otherwise.

On patrol Chapman tangled with a swarm of German fighters and was rescued only after a group of his own comrades pulled him to safety. That same day he went up again, this time alone, and returned with a bloody head and a bullet-ridden plane. A week later, his head still bandaged, he flew into a Fokker formation and was shot down. Chapman was the first member of an American combat unit to be killed in World War I.

Norman Prince, whose idea launched the Lafayette

Escadrille, died when his Nieuport flew into an electric power line. He had officially downed five enemy craft, and his friends testified that he should have been credited with many more. On his deathbed Prince was awarded the Legion of Honor medal; he had already won the Medaille Militaire and the Croix de Guerre.

Lufbery, French-American Hero

ONE OF the most famous fliers in the Lafayette Escadrille was a naturalized American who fought with the American Air Service after the escadrille came to an end. Raoul Gervais Lufbery died in 1918 when he leaped from his blazing Nieuport to escape being burned alive.

Until that time Lufbery seemed to lead a charmed life, his days full of adventure. Born in France, he was left alone as a small boy when his mother died and his father remarried. Raoul and his two brothers were reared by their grandmother. In his teens Raoul set out to find his father, now in America.

Raoul never did find his father. But he roamed around the United States a good bit, then joined the U.S. Army. His service qualified him for American citizenship. Duly sworn as a citizen, and out of the army, he sailed for the Far East.

In Indochina Lufbery met Marc Pourpé, a pioneer pilot who was giving exhibitions in his Bleriot monoplane. The two became friends at once, and Lufbery went to work for Pourpé as his one-man ground crew. For the next couple of years they went from place to place in Europe and Africa, seeking crowds who would pay something to watch Pourpé stunt-fly the Bleriot.

Pourpé and Lufbery were in France to buy a new airplane when World War I erupted. Pourpé joined the French air arm at once. Lufbery could fight for France and still keep his U.S. citizenship only by joining the French Foreign Legion. So he did, and was at once posted to Pourpé's squadron as an aviation mechanic.

Three months later Pourpé was shot down. Lufbery's sadness was deep but silent. He went about his work servicing planes, he drank heavily in his free time, and he never spoke of his loss. Nevertheless his superiors sensed his grief. The only way they could help was to accept his application for pilot training.

Lufbery learned to fly by using the clumsy Farman and Voisin two-seater observation planes as his aerial classrooms. He wasn't a very good student, and when he won his wings he was sent to a bomber squadron, not the fighter unit he preferred. But when the Escadrille Americaine (later to become the Lafayette) was formed, Lufbery was one of the first to join it.

It took a while for Lufbery to accustom himself to the Nieuport fighters. Two months went by before he downed his first German plane, but he got his second win that same afternoon. The victories came after a relentless daily program of pursuing the enemy, staying in the air until either his fuel or his ammunition was nearly gone. Chalking up his fifth hit, he became an ace on October 12, 1916, when he knocked down an Aviatik directly over a German gun factory.

Becoming an ace, with all the fame and attention that went with it, gave Lufbery added confidence in himself. Now that Norman Prince was dead, he was the leading pilot in the escadrille. He felt a responsibility to his squadron, to his adopted country, America, and to the memory of his friend Pourpé. Once he was sent to Nice, a resort town on the Mediterranean, to seek some relief from recurring muscle aches. He returned to his squadron before his prescribed rest period was up.

Some time after the United States entered the war in April 1917, the Lafayette Escadrille was disbanded. Most of its members were sent to the newly formed American Air Service, a branch of the U.S. Signal Corps. Lufbery was posted to an American training group with the rank of major in January 1918. He had shot down sixteen enemy planes, he had been in the thick of the fighting for three years, and he rebelled against this backwater duty.

After three months he got what he wanted: a position as instructor with the 94th Aero Squadron moving into the Champagne sector of the fighting front. The 94th had Nieuport fighters, all right, but no guns. After futilely "going through channels" for several weeks, Lufbery went directly to General John J. Pershing, top U.S. commander in Europe. He got his guns.

As instructor, Lufbery was calm, thorough. He coached his pilots to keep their heads in case of fire aboard the plane: keep the fire away from the wind; land as soon as possible. Don't jump clear, he warned; you'll have no chance to survive. But Lufbery failed to follow his own orders.

On May 19, 1918, Lufbery met and mixed with an Albatros right over the 94th's airfield at Toul. The Albatros's shell hit Lufbery's gas tank, and at once the Nieuport was almost swallowed up in flames. As the Americans of the 94th watched in horror, Lufbery left his cockpit, climbed out on a wing, and jumped. Searchers located his scorched body in a nearby garden. He was entirely covered with flowers.

Bill Thaw, Escadrille Ace

BILL THAW was a young American socialite who served a hitch in the Lafayette Escadrille before going over to the American Air Service. He was the kind of American that the Lafayette group seemed to attract: rich, romantic, adventurous. Lufbery had been, by contrast, an exception—a naturalized American who knew little about his adopted country, a poor young man who spoke English haltingly.

Thaw was born in Pittsburgh, the son of a banker. His mother was a well-known art collector. The boy went to prep schools in the East and spent two years at Yale. At nineteen he learned to fly at Glenn Curtiss's school in Hammondsport, New York. He soon made headlines by flying from Newport, Rhode Island, to New York City by way of New Haven, Connecticut. He didn't stop until he had flown under all four East River bridges and around the Statue of Liberty.

In the spring before World War I started, Bill Thaw was in France, flying a Curtiss Jenny along the Mediterranean coast. The French liked him and made him a member of the French Aero Club. In August 1914 he was trying to sell the French government an automatic stabilizer for aircraft that he had helped invent. War came, and Thaw joined the French Foreign Legion.

Assigned to an infantry unit, Thaw chafed at not being able to fly. He finally wangled his way into a military flight training outfit. First he flew in Deperdussin two-seaters, armed with a carbine and a pistol. Then he trained in Caudron two-seaters, which he flew with student observers.

Thaw heard about the new Escadrille Americaine, but he wasn't much interested. He continued to fly Caudrons and Nieuports in a French squadron until Norman Prince finally coaxed him into becoming a member of his escadrille. Once in, Thaw was a superb trainer and leader of American fliers. He wanted them to survive aerial combat, and he taught them every known way to do so. He knocked down five enemy aircraft himself and became an ace.

When the Lafayette Escadrille disbanded, Thaw became a major in the American Air Service, not a bad rank for a pilot who was only twenty-three. He headed the 103rd Aero Squadron and later the Third Pursuit Group. By the end of the war Thaw was a lieutenant colonel, winner of the Distinguished Service Cross, Legion of Honor, and Croix de Guerre.

After the war Thaw kept his interest in aviation while engaging in various businesses. In 1928 he was a copilot flying a Lockheed Vega in an across-the-U.S. race. On the way the plane crashed and Thaw was severely hurt. He died in 1934.

Most of the Americans who were killed while flying for the Lafayette Escadrille are buried in a memorial of that name near Versailles, just outside Paris. The shrine was dedicated on July 4, 1928. It is made up of a central arch flanked by colonnades leading to a burial crypt. There are thirteen stained-glass windows showing the pilots in flight over their battle sectors. Despite political differences between France and the United States over the years, the memorial serves to remind both the French and the Americans of a friendship that must remain alive.

CHAPTER **7**
AMERICAN ACES IN WORLD WAR I

FRANK LUKE, EDDIE RICKENBACKER

In 1916 Woodrow Wilson was elected to a second term as President of the United States. His catchy campaign slogan was, "He kept us out of war." World War I had been raging in Europe for more than two years. The combatants on the Eastern and Western Fronts were locked in a giant struggle. Millions of troops on both sides fought from trenches, where gains or losses were measured in feet or yards of territory taken or retaken. Despite such limited progress or loss, the dead and wounded were hauled away by the thousands.

The United States tried hard not to become involved, even though in 1915 a British passenger ship, the *Lusitania*, had been sunk by a German submarine, or U-boat, off the Irish coast. Among the 1,198 passengers who drowned were 124 Americans. The outraged voice of neutral America forced Germany to restrict its submarine attacks on passenger ships—for a time.

Then in January 1917 Germany announced that its U-boat fleet would attack all neutral and Allied shipping on the high seas. With that, the United States cut off all diplomatic ties to Germany. (The German ambassador who had protested the name "Escadrille Americaine" was sent home at once.)

Less than three months later the American public learned that U-boats had sunk four U.S. ships. The result was predictable. Abandoning neutrality, Wilson called a special session of Congress to ask for a declaration of war against Germany. Congress acted on April 6, 1917.

Then and only then did real war preparations begin. The United States had to start from scratch in mustering men, munitions, supplies, aircraft. And in those days there were no jet planes to furnish swift transportation, no satellites to offer instant worldwide communications, no computers to organize and keep track of the flow of thousands of items needed to fight a war. Long-distance phones were slow and cranky; there were no electronic typewriters; even the training films were silent.

Thus it was no wonder that the United States was slow in getting started. The wonder was that it acted as fast as it did. Military plane production was one program that lagged. Congress voted what was then (and still is) the immense sum of $640,000,000 to build 22,625 planes and train the men to fly and repair them.

But from Kitty Hawk until this time American industry had actually built only about a thousand aircraft of all kinds. It simply did not have the engineering and industrial experience to produce planes in such vast numbers in so short a time.

To overcome the plane shortage quickly, the United States decided to buy Spads and Nieuports, the best-known fighter planes, from the French. At home it would concentrate on building trainers, mainly the Curtiss Jenny, and observation planes, mainly the British-designed De Havilland.

As for pilots and mechanics, there were plenty of eager volunteers, some 38,000 of them, who wanted to enlist. These men had to be trained in a hurry; the war wasn't going to wait for them. Pilot training was divided into three phases: ground, primary, and advanced.

Ground instruction was offered at eight college campuses, where about 23,000 would-be fliers took the course. About three fourths of them passed and went on to primary flight training. This took place at various military airfields around the country.

The airfields were new, the flight instructors green, the Jennys available for teaching few in number. It was a minor miracle that so many men honestly qualified for advanced instruction. At first these advanced students were sent over to Britain, France, and Italy for training. There the instructors were more experienced and the planes more like those used in actual fighting.

Soon more Americans showed up for advanced schooling in Europe than could be handled. So the air service had to provide its own training in the United States. It hurriedly set up air bases around the country, each with tents for housing the students and with canvas hangars for the training planes. It was all done hastily, with enormous pressure exerted to get pilots into the air against the enemy immediately. All told, about 10,000 pilots were graduated from these advanced-training bases.

By the fall of 1917 hundreds of barely qualified pilots were on their way to France. A similar program had taught mechanics the care and feeding of military aircraft, and they too were off to France. (A total of about 10,000 aircraft mechanics were trained in this program.)

In fields outside Paris the American pilots were taught to fly the French way. They studied fighter-plane flying by rolling around the ground in a single seater with its wings clipped. They practiced gunnery in the air, using Nieuports modified for teaching purposes.

If they were stationed in Paris, the American fliers congregated at the Hotel de Crillon on the Place de la Concord during their free time. Virtually all of them were in their early twenties or even younger. Like all young people, they liked parties and good times. But all of them saw the weekly casualty reports. Behind their party-going gaiety was the realization that each of them stood a good chance of ending up as a statistic on one of those casualty lists.

Frank Luke, Medal of Honor Winner

FRANK LUKE fought as though he knew he would be killed before the war was over. He was right: he was killed—but not before he had downed fifteen enemy balloons and six aircraft. For his valor, Luke was awarded the Congressional Medal of Honor, one of the few won by American airmen in World War I.

Luke was a loner who hated to be around other people and who had no sense of humor at all. When the United States entered the war, Luke's first thought was to keep out of the service. He wanted no part of the discipline of army life. But his sister became a Red Cross nurse, and his brother joined the field artillery. Reluctantly Luke enlisted in the Signal Corps and asked to be assigned to an aviation unit.

Qualifying as a pilot, Luke was in France by March 1918. He was posted to the 27th Aero Squadron based near Château-Thierry, scene of one of the bloodiest battles of World War I. Almost at once his solitary and rebellious nature began to show.

He disliked flying in formation as his squadron went out on patrol. Often he took off on his own and went hunting for the enemy. One day in August 1918 Luke had just parted company with his squadron when he spotted six Albatros fighters in formation over their own airfield. Coolly he picked off one and shot it down. Because the enemy plane fell behind its own lines, Luke had no witness to confirm his victory and so could not claim it on his record.

Among the targets that Allied airmen were instructed to attack were the enemy's tethered, or captive, balloons. These observation balloons, linked to the ground by long cables, acted as the "eyes" of the artillery. The observer in the balloon basket signaled the cannoneers when hits were scored and where further firing would be most effective. The balloons were a menace to Allied ground troops and a legitimate target for Allied planes. The balloons, of course, were protected by their own aircraft; they were not just sitting ducks.

Members of the 27th talked a good deal about the possibility of shooting down balloons, and Frank Luke decided to try his luck against them. He took off in a Spad and went hunting, just as he had done as a boy in Arizona. He sighted one, but was himself spotted at the same time. The balloon was hauled down by its cable almost to the ground, but Luke dived again and again at it. Finally his bullets pierced its hydrogen-filled bag, or envelope, and the balloon was swallowed up in flames.

Luke reported his victory to his commander, who then

decided to let him go after as many balloons as he could find. Luke asked that a new friend, Lieutenant Joe Wehner, fly along with him to draw off enemy fire and generally act as guard and lookout. The two had met only recently, but a strong friendship had grown up between them. This was unusual for Luke; he didn't like most people.

Luke and Wehner set off on a balloon-busting campaign. Daily they searched for their targets, and it was a rare day that they did not return with a confirmed kill. On September 18, 1918, they were on their way home after knocking down two balloons. They met a flight of Fokkers, whose pilots attacked at once. Luke downed one, then another, and looked around to see how Wehner was doing. Seeing no sign of his partner, he tore into another Fokker, sent it crashing to earth, then headed for his base.

Wehner never returned. Luke brooded over the loss of his friend until he was sent on leave to Paris for a few days. He came back early, demanding more balloon assignments. He was given a new wing man to replace Wehner, a lieutenant named Ivan Roberts. On their very first flight together they tangled with five Fokkers, and Roberts was shot down. Luke scored a direct hit, but barely made it back to the base.

In his dark and silent way Luke grieved as well over Roberts's death. One night he took off without permission and returned the next day. Asked where he'd been, he said simply that he had gone to visit the Storks Squadron at their base. And, he added, he had shot down another balloon.

His commander grounded him for this act of defiance. Luke paid no attention to the grounding. He went aloft at once, hunting for three balloons he had located the day before. He got the three balloons and headed for home, knowing he'd be court-martialed for his disobedience.

Before he could return to base, antiaircraft guns knocked him out of the sky. He crash-landed and got out of his cockpit dizzy, shaken, but apparently unharmed. A platoon of German infantrymen surrounded him, but Luke did not want to surrender. He blazed away with his pistol against the advancing soldiers. They returned fire and killed him.

The date was September 29, 1918. World War I was to end six weeks later.

Captain Eddie, Leading U.S. Ace

ANOTHER CONGRESSIONAL Medal of Honor winner, the American ace of aces, lived a spectacular life before, during, and long after World War I. He was Edward Vernon Rickenbacker, the renowned "Captain Eddie."

The air service as well as the Lafayette Escadrille seemed to attract the well-born sons of well-to-do American families. But Frank Luke was a poor boy for all of his short life. And Eddie Rickenbacker started out poor but managed to accumulate a considerable fortune during his long career.

Born in Columbus, Ohio, Rickenbacker was the son of immigrants from Switzerland who spelled their name Richenbacher. (During World War I Rickenbacker Americanized the spelling to avoid being called a German spy.) Eddie, the third of eight children, grew up in a four-room house his father had built all by himself. The Rickenbacker kids raised vegetables, chickens, pigs, and goats for their milk.

The family spoke German at home. Young Eddie spoke English only at school, and that with a strong accent. His schoolmates called him Dutchy, or Kraut.

"I had to fight my way into school in the morning, stand up for myself at recess, and fight my way home again after school," he later recalled. He also fought often with his older brother, Bill, simply because Eddie couldn't bear to be second best in anything. Throughout his long lifetime he was always an intense competitor.

Eddie was thirteen when his father was killed by a pile driver. The boy dropped out of the seventh grade and went to work. He ran through a series of jobs, leaving each after a few months to seek more money and the start of a real career. He finally found his career job in a local garage, but he had to accept beginner's pay: 75 cents a day.

At fifteen, Eddie enrolled in a course in mechanical and automotive engineering with a good correspondence school. This, plus his garage experience, got him a job with a new automobile plant in Columbus. He rose rapidly from sweeper to design engineer.

In 1906 his company entered three cars in the Vanderbilt Cup race to be held on Long Island, New York. Eddie was chosen to ride in one car, acting as mechanic for the driver—who happened to be the company owner.

In the qualifying trials their car's engine failed, and they were eliminated. The other two cars lost out in the finals, and the $50,000 spent on race preparations was lost. Nevertheless, the company owner's liking for young Rickenbacker grew. When he left his own company to take a post as chief engineer for a larger automotive concern, he took the youth with him.

Rickenbacker began by testing new cars before they were shipped to the dealers. Soon he was accompanying the shipments, making sure the cars would operate when sold from the dealers' showrooms. Then he began demonstrating his dealers' cars by driving them in local auto races. Finally he quit his job and became a full-time race driver. He entered big contests all over the country and won many of them.

As a race driver Rickenbacker's name and bank account grew. He set a race-car speed record of 134 miles an hour and in more than one prewar year won over $35,000 in prizes. Before the United States entered the war in 1917 Rickenbacker urged the air service to set up a fighter squadron of race drivers. He argued that such men were quick to act and react at high speeds under stress and would make fine combat pilots. His proposal was turned down.

When war came, Rickenbacker enlisted, first serving as chauffeur to Colonel William Mitchell, head of the air service. Mitchell soon allowed him to enter flight school and qualify as a pilot.

Rickenbacker was first assigned as engineering officer for the squadrons based at Issoudun. The air service wanted to keep him there permanently to take advantage of his vast mechanical skills. But in his free time, Rickenbacker went up in Nieuports to learn more about flying. Later he was sent to gunnery school, then assigned to the 94th Aero Squadron. Raoul Lufbery was the squadron commander.

At first Rickenbacker did not get along with the other pilots in the 94th. Most of them were "gentlemen," and he was a rough-talking, hard-driving, grade-school dropout. At twenty-eight he was also somewhat older than his fellow pilots. Gradually Rickenbacker learned to get along with them and they with him.

Captain Eddie Rickenbacker, Congressional Medal of Honor winner, points out "Hat in the Ring" squadron emblem on his Nieuport plane.

Rickenbacker's first flying partner was James Norman Hall, who would later be coauthor of the classic *Mutiny on the Bounty*. With Hall, Rickenbacker scored his first kill against a Pfalz fighter. Later Hall himself was shot down and taken prisoner. Rickenbacker took Hall's place as flight commander.

About this time Rickenbacker was stricken with a severe earache. The ailment proved to be mastoiditis. He was operated on and spent two months recovering. When he returned he found many of his friends gone—killed, wounded, taken prisoner. Casualties were increasing because the new Fokkers were better planes than the aging Nieuports the Americans had to use.

Rickenbacker studied how to survive in a Nieuport. He saw that many of his friends crashed to their deaths when they put their Nieuports into a steep dive—the wings ripped away from the fuselage. One time it almost happened to him. He had shot down an Albatros and was coming back to level flight. Suddenly his top right wing collapsed and the canvas coating blew away. Rickenbacker had to use all of his considerable skill to baby his plane back to the base.

On May 30, 1918, Rickenbacker downed his fifth plane and became an ace. About that time the Air Service was removed from the U.S. Signal Corps and set up on its own. The 94th was linked with other units to form the First Pursuit Group. And in August the group's Nieuports were replaced by Spads. Rickenbacker liked the new plane, especially the way it could climb fast. He put the Spad through its paces, noting its weaknesses and its strengths.

In September 1918 Rickenbacker was made commander of the 94th Aero Squadron. His leadership ability had been finally recognized; everybody had known all along that he was an excellent engineer and a fine combat pilot, relentless in pursuit of the foe.

By the end of October Rickenbacker's score had risen to twenty-six kills, all confirmed. His squadron companions knew that he should have been credited with at least a dozen more. Now the war was almost over. The November 11 Armistice loomed just ahead.

But Rickenbacker's notable career had just begun. After the war, he went on to new achievements as an executive with several automobile companies and as principal owner of the Indianapolis Speedway, on which he had raced several times before the war. For twenty-one years he was president of Eastern Air Lines.

In 1942, less than a year after the United States entered World War II, Rickenbacker almost lost his life. On a secret mission for Secretary of War Henry Stimson, Rickenbacker in his plane was forced down into the Pacific Ocean, about 600 miles north of Samoa. He and seven others drifted on rubber rafts for twenty-four days before they were picked up.

The World War I ace left his imprint on World War II as well.

CHAPTER 8
MITCHELL AND THE FIGHT FOR AIR FORCE RECOGNITION

The Allied nations, many historians say, brought World War I to a victorious end partly because of their growing air power. After four bloody and exhausting years of trench warfare, it was the Allied pilots who broke the enemies' hold and drove them back toward Germany. Allied fliers, many of them Americans, enabled Allied ground troops to triumph. Military aviation had come of age by the end of World War I.

But after the war a number of American generals and admirals refused to accept the recognition airplanes had earned in combat. "Victories on land are achieved by the foot soldier slugging it out with the enemy," they said. "Wars at sea are won by the big combat vessels, especially the battleships. Airplanes only kill each other off and have no effect on our drive to victory."

Billy Mitchell—Martyr?

THIS ATTITUDE persisted for years after World War I was over, lingering almost until the start of World War II. In the 1920s one man sacrificed his career in army aviation to attack this attitude. In doing so, he rallied around him the supporters who eventually created the U.S. Air Force. The man's name was General William Mitchell.

Known affectionately as Billy, William Mitchell was born in Nice, France. His wealthy young parents were living in Europe at the time. Billy's father, John, had inherited a fortune from his father, Alexander, a banker and one of the founders of Milwaukee, Wisconsin.

When Billy was old enough to start school, his parents brought him back to Milwaukee. At first Billy's schoolmates joshed him about his French accent. He soon forgot his French and learned to talk like his friends.

The Mitchells settled down on a 400-acre estate, Meadowmere, in Milwaukee County. John Mitchell raised cattle and bred racehorses. Billy grew up learning to ride with easy grace, to shoot a rifle and shotgun accurately, and to find rare birds, which he killed, stuffed, and presented to the Milwaukee Museum.

Even as a boy Billy was supremely self-confident. He always knew what he wanted to do and where he wanted to go.

When Billy was seventeen, John Mitchell was elected U.S. Senator from Wisconsin. The family moved to Washington, D.C., and Billy enrolled in the capital's George Washington University. Before he could begin classes, the Spanish-American War broke out in April 1898. Billy promptly enlisted in the First Wisconsin Regiment.

Private Mitchell was with his regiment in Florida, awaiting transport to the fighting in Cuba. While waiting, he was ordered back to Washington to accept a commission as second lieutenant in the U.S. Signal Corps. General Adolphus Greely, the Signal Corps chief, had heard of Billy (very likely from Senator John Mitchell) and considered him officer material, even though he was only eighteen.

The war was over by December 1898, and Billy arrived in Cuba too late for the shooting. He did serve there as a member of the occupation army. His job from January to June 1899 was to direct a work party of forty men as they strung 140 miles of telegraph line around the island.

The job done, and done well, Mitchell was transferred to another former Spanish possession, the Philippine Islands, taken over by the United States as a result of the war. There, fighting still raged between American troops and Filipino insurgents. Despite this, Mitchell set up a telegraph system on Luzon, the major Philippine island.

Then General Greely tagged Mitchell to do the same job in Alaska. All army outposts in Alaska were to be linked by telegraph. Mitchell tackled the job with his usual vigor and selfassurance. Before, such work had been done only in the short Alaska summer. When winter came, the Signal Corps soldiers retired to their barracks and did virtually nothing.

Mitchell put them to work summer and winter, and the men welcomed the activity. Mitchell found that in summer the pack mules and horses sank deep into the swamps and mud and could carry only light loads on their backs. But in winter the animals could pull heavy sledges over the packed snow. Using such ingenious approaches Mitchell made his difficult task easier.

The Alaska job was done by 1903. Mitchell was now a captain, although he was still shy of twenty-four. A series of Signal Corps assignments took him over much of the world. He was back home when war erupted in 1914. At once he began to watch what the British, French, and Germans were doing with their aircraft. Mitchell was convinced that air power could make the difference between victory and defeat.

Mitchell's interest in this was very personal: American military aviation was under the wing of the Signal Corps, Mitchell's own outfit. And Mitchell wanted desperately to be a part of the Signal Corps air program, even though in 1914 it consisted of only twenty-eight planes, and not all of these were airworthy.

Mitchell took flying lessons and prepared himself to be an active air commander. In 1917 he went to Europe to observe the war firsthand. He arrived in March; in April the United States declared war on Germany and the Central Powers. Soon Mitchell paid a call on General John J. Pershing, head of the American Expeditionary Force (AEF), at his Paris headquarters.

Mitchell, then a major, proceeded to tell General Pershing just how his Signal Corps planes could work with American infantry and artillery. Pershing, somewhat taken aback by this confident young major, was soon won over by the force of Mitchell's presentation.

Major General Hugh Trenchard, Britain's aviation chief in France, also received a call from Mitchell. Trenchard told him of Britain's program to develop formation flights instead of sending individual planes up to seek out the enemy. Trenchard revealed plans to send bomber planes deep into Germany, there to bomb munitions factories and supply depots. Mitchell saw ways in which America's air power could work with Britain's.

But Mitchell had to wait months before the first American pilots were trained and sailed for France. And the thousands of planes that the United States had planned to manufacture immediately? No American combat plane appeared in France while the war was still on. The only American-built aircraft to be delivered to France were a few hundred De Havilland observation planes. The Americans had to do their fighting and flying in French and British aircraft.

Thus it was well into 1918 before U.S. pilots were flying against the foe in any great numbers. Mitchell fumed at the delay. He often went up in his own Spad to have a look around and get a sense of what his pilots later were to experience.

On May 27, 1918, Mitchell suffered a keen personal loss. His younger brother John was killed in an air accident in France. Mitchell's diary entry for that day reads:

"As he came in to land he had a great deal of speed. His front wheels hit hard and he bounced. . . . Apparently he decided to make another turn of the field, so he put on his motor and started to make a circle.

"When he started to make the turn, the longerons or beams in the back part of the fuselage broke, and the ship fell to earth, and he was instantly killed. . . .

"Thus died my only brother, a splendid young man of twenty-tnree. . . . He had everything in him that a brother should have. . . ."

Mitchell had little time for grieving. Pershing had appointed a top commander for the entire air service in France, and Mitchell in effect was demoted. But he followed orders and went ahead with plans for the big air assaults at Château-Thierry and St.-Mihiel.

That summer the air drives, coordinated with ground troop movements, were highly successful, and thousands of German soldiers surrendered. On November 11 the war was over, and the Allied world rejoiced. Even many defeated Germans were secretly thankful that the killing had stopped.

But for Billy Mitchell a new war had begun: a war to make the army and navy commanders, the U.S. government, and the American people accept air power as a vital part of national defense. He fought that war with every weapon at his command.

These weapons included logic and forceful argument. They did not include diplomacy, subtlety, compromise, or even tact. Mitchell preached what was on his mind and in his heart. He would not back off; he would not be silenced. Because of this sense of mission, he sometimes went too far.

The first real test of Mitchell's arguments for air power came in 1921. The *Ostfriesland* had to be sunk. This was the battleship handed over to the Allies by defeated Germany. Under the treaty, the ship could not be used by any of the victorious Allies. It had to be destroyed, and it was up to the United States to do it.

Many experts considered the *Ostfriesland* unsinkable. It was a 27,000-ton ship with eighty-five watertight compartments, a triple hull, and a coating of hardened steel armor. In the war it had taken many direct hits from Allied big guns. It had also struck a mine that would have demolished a lesser ship. From these the *Ostfriesland* had escaped without serious damage.

Mitchell demanded that his air service bombers be allowed to demonstrate their ability to sink the German battleship. U.S. Army and Navy officials reluctantly gave their consent. The *Ostfriesland* was towed to an isolated area in Chesapeake Bay, and all crew left the ship.

Standing nearby was the U.S. battleship *Pennsylvania*, ready to fire round after round from its 14-inch guns to sink its former foe if the aerial bombs failed. And many spectators aboard the transport ship *Henderson* watching the show were betting that the air assault would fail.

The *Pennsylvania* never got a chance to fire a round. Mitchell sent a fleet of six Martin bombers plus a Handley-Page over the target. Each dropped a 2,000-pound bomb. Slowly, slowly, slowly the *Ostfriesland*, like a giant dying whale, slipped beneath the surface. Within minutes it was at the bottom of Chesapeake Bay.

Mitchell had proved one point: planes could sink a battleship. But Mitchell went on to argue that battleships were thus obsolete. This did not happen to be true at the time. U.S. battleships served effectively in World War II. They bombarded the shores of enemy-held territory before American troops fought their way ashore. The battleships' big guns continued to fire over the heads of the U.S. invaders moving inland.

It is true that today the few existing U.S. battleships are mothballed and are likely to remain so. But they served twenty-five years after Mitchell was ready to condemn them.

But Mitchell kept on campaigning. Most of all he wanted in the early 1920s what actually took place in 1947. This was the creation of a cabinet-level Department of Defense and under it three co-equal branches: the Departments of the Army, the Navy, and the Air Force. Only in this way, Mitchell argued, could military aviation do its best work.

In 1923 Mitchell married for the second time. The couple took their honeymoon in the Pacific, where Mitchell was ordered to look into U.S. air activities in Hawaii and the Philippines.

In Hawaii he discovered an alarming situation. The U.S. Army and Navy absolutely refused to work together in setting up island defenses. The hostility was so great that their top commanders even declined to attend the same parties.

Mitchell continued writing and speaking, pounding home the same basic points: a separate air force must be created; armies must serve under an air force; the battleship is obsolete; antiaircraft fire doesn't work; the navy can't guard our coast against attack by enemy planes; and so on. All this, remember, while he was still on active duty, a brigadier general and assistant chief of air service, who had to obey orders from his superiors.

Most of Mitchell's charges came true much later. At the time, however, many seemed reckless and unfounded. So the War Department began to crack down on him. His term as assistant chief of air service was up in 1925, and he was not reappointed.

And he could no longer claim the rank of brigadier general that went with the post. He had to accept the lesser rank of colonel. He was ordered out of Washington to take up duties as air officer with the Eighth Corps at Fort Sam Houston in San Antonio, Texas. He took the demotion and the move without grumbling.

But soon after he reported to Fort Sam Houston, an air tragedy stunned the nation and got Billy Mitchell

General William Mitchell led the fight for recognition of air power as vital to national defense. His fight was won long after his death.

fighting mad. The tragedy was the destruction of the U.S. Navy dirigible *Shenandoah*, with the loss of fourteen lives.

"Son" of the German zeppelins, the *Shenandoah* was the first rigid airship built in the United States. Its 680-foot-long envelope, shaped like a cigar, held nineteen separate gas bags filled with helium. Engines, propellers, and crew were housed in two gondolas hanging from the underbelly of the envelope. The navy built it to serve at sea, to act as a lookout for the fleet.

But in September 1925 the *Shenandoah* was given a public relations assignment. This was to fly over state fairs in the Midwest and give the people a chance—a first chance for many of them—to see the navy in action. The *Shenandoah*'s captain, Zachary Landsdowne, protested the assignment. He knew how to handle his airship during hazardous climatic conditions over the sea. But he feared the tricky September weather inland, with its thunderstorms and tornadoes.

Landsdowne's fears were tragically justified. Over Ohio, the *Shenandoah* ran into an electric storm combined with tornadoes. The dirigible was ripped apart, gutted. In one gondola fourteen men, including Landsdowne, were killed. The other gondola, holding twenty-eight men, broke free and floated to safety.

News of the *Shenandoah* disaster and the Navy Department's wishy-washy apology for it aroused Mitchell to a white-hot fury. He released a seventeen-page statement to the press, saying at one point, "These accidents are the direct result of the incompetency, criminal negligence, and almost treasonable administration of the national defense by the Navy and War Departments."

He also accused the nonflying officers of the army and navy of giving airmen obsolete, unworkable, and downright dangerous equipment to handle. His accusations were harsh, extreme, but with strong elements of truth in them.

Within days Mitchell was ordered to appear before the President's Aircraft Board in Washington. At that hearing, Mitchell offered a scathing indictment of conditions in military aviation. He damned the few planes, the outmoded tools and repair facilities, the inadequate number of qualified pilots. He warned that the United States was pitifully unprepared for the next war, which was sure to be fought mainly in the air.

The Aircraft Board also listened to the testimony of a number of old-line generals and admirals. They said that airplanes were fine for scouting and observation during battle but had little further use. As was to be expected, the Aircraft Board sided with the generals and admirals. The

Board's report concluded: "We do not consider that air power, as an arm of the national defense, has yet demonstrated its value."

Most of the army's and the navy's active pilots were behind Mitchell. Much of the public was, too. So he had a great deal of popular support when the War Department decided to try him in a general court-martial. Mitchell chose Congressman Frank Reid to defend him. Reid was an expert on military aviation and the best choice for a defense attorney.

The trial board was made up of ten high-ranking army officers, one of whom was Douglas MacArthur. For seven weeks the trial went on, with each side offering important evidence. In the end Mitchell lost. His rank and pay were suspended, and he was relieved of all duty for five years. The verdict meant that Mitchell was still in the army, but he had been silenced.

Mitchell would not accept the verdict. He still had the right to resign from the army, and he did. For years he made fiery speeches and wrote critical magazine articles, keeping the public aware of his war with the War Department.

When Franklin D. Roosevelt was elected President in 1932, the air service became the semi-independent U.S. Army Air Corps. Mitchell had hopes of being chosen as assistant secretary for air in the War Department. He had several interviews with the new President, but he never got the appointment.

Mitchell continued to speak out, testifying often before several congressional committees. He traveled all over the world, and when he was home on his Virginia estate he was forever riding, fishing, shooting. He was an active man who never knew how to slow down. The end came suddenly in 1936. He died of a heart attack at the age of fifty-five.

But Billy Mitchell lives on—in the Department of Defense created from his plans, in the full acceptance of air power by the U.S. government and the American people, and in the peacetime defenses against a future war.

CHAPTER
FLYING THE ATLANTIC
ALCOCK/BROWN, CHARLES LINDBERGH

Only a scant ten years after the Wright brothers took to the air, a rich prize was offered to the first flying team to cross the Atlantic. In 1913 Lord Northcliffe, publisher of the British newspaper *The Daily Mail*, guaranteed a sum of 10,000 pounds—then equal to about $50,000 in U.S. money—to the pilots who would do this. Northcliffe figured the task would be too great for a lone pilot to tackle. It would take two fliers, perhaps three.

Nor was Northcliffe expecting a nonstop flight. The best planes of the day were simply incapable of flying more than a few hundred miles without landing. So the contest rules provided that the plane could set down on the ocean and be refueled by an escort ship.

Even with this provision, no pilots were brash enough to accept Northcliffe's challenge. World War I soon intervened, and all thought of competing for the prize was set aside. Aviation made giant strides during the war. Designers and builders outdid themselves to improve air speed, distance, maneuverability, safety. What they accomplished in wartime would have taken many more years in time of peace.

When the war ended, Vickers Ltd., a British aircraft manufacturer, was building a plane that seemed ready to claim the Northcliffe prize—even though the new rules demanded a nonstop flight. The Vickers Vimy was a two-seater biplane with a wingspan of more than 67 feet. It was powered by twin 12-cylinder Rolls-Royce engines, each of 360 horsepower. With the wartime bomb racks out and extra gasoline tanks installed, the Vimy's designers figured it could fly from Newfoundland to Ireland. This shortest route across the Atlantic measured about 1,880 miles.

Jack Alcock and Teddie Brown

VICKERS WAS looking hard for a pilot to fly the Vimy across the ocean when one likely candidate presented himself. He was John "Jack" Alcock, age twenty-eight, recently a captain in the Royal Air Force. Alcock had been around airplanes for ten years or more, starting out as an aircraft mechanic and flying bombing missions during the war. He was a fine choice for pilot.

Now Vickers needed a navigator. A few weeks after Alcock was hired, another ex-RAF officer named Arthur Whitten ("Teddie") Brown applied for this job. Brown had been an aerial observer whose plane had crashed behind German lines. A prisoner of war for many months, Brown had suffered a leg injury in the crash that left him with a permanent limp. This did not interfere with his navigation skills, and Brown was soon teamed up with Alcock.

By the spring of 1919 several other aircraft firms were also ready to compete for the Northcliffe prize, now increased to 13,000 pounds. One aspiring ocean-hopper testflew his plane off the New Jersey shore and soon dunked into the sea. Another took off from England and was only 22 miles out when he had to ditch his plane in the water.

The other contestants figured that west-to-east winds would be in their favor. So they dismantled their planes, put them aboard freighters, and sailed for St. John's, Newfoundland, off Canada's east coast. There they began hacking out airfields from the rugged terrain. They needed runways at least 300 yards long for takeoffs.

Alcock and Brown were the last of four competing teams to arrive in Newfoundland. One by one, the others dropped out, either crashing on takeoff or going down at sea. One never took off at all. After a desperate search, Alcock and Brown finally found a stretch of 500 yards that could be leveled off for their flight. On June 14, 1919, the field in shape, their plane fine-tuned, they took off with the wind at their back.

The flight was a hard one. They ran into fog, clouds, ice, snow, treacherous crosswinds. At one point they were flying upside down only 50 feet above the water. Instruments failed. The engine exhaust pipe ripped away, leaving pilot and navigator exposed to the fumes.

But they made it. After 16 hours and 28 minutes in the air, they nosed down into an Irish bog. They were the first to cross the Atlantic by air, and all honors were heaped on them. Winston Churchill, in those days Secretary of State for War and Air, presented them with the Northcliffe prize of 13,000 pounds. King George V conferred knighthood on them. Each could thereafter affix "Sir" to his name.

Only six months later Alcock died as he attempted to land at a fogbound French airfield. Brown quit flying and lived on to old age.

Lucky Lindy

THE NEXT great prize to dazzle the aviation world was one offered by Raymond Orteig, a New York City hotel owner of French nationality. He would present $25,000 to the first man or men who flew nonstop from New York to Paris, or from Paris to New York, a distance of some 3,600 miles. A young airmail pilot named Charles A. Lindbergh won the Orteig prize in 1927 for his solo flight.

Unknown until then, Lindbergh earned instant and lasting fame for his feat. It was a fame he had not sought, and he was always uncomfortable with it. At one later point in life, fame brought tragedy: his infant firstborn child was kidnapped and murdered. At another later point, his reputation suffered serious damage: he was accused of being too friendly to the Nazi German government and its chief, Adolf Hitler. But Lindbergh kept on working in aviation and eventually flew into calmer skies.

Charles Augustus Lindbergh, Jr.—"Slim" to his old friends, "Lindy" to the worldwide public who wildly acclaimed him after his solo span of the Atlantic—was born in Detroit, Michigan. His father was a Minnesota lawyer who later served five terms in Congress. His mother was a high school science teacher. (Later the two quietly separated but were never legally divorced.)

Young Lindbergh grew up in Little Falls, Minnesota. He also spent several winters in Washington, D.C., when his father was a congressman. The boy often visited his mother's father in Detroit. He was C. H. Land, a dentist and inventor, who taught Charles to use the tools and instruments in his workroom and let him experiment with his chemicals.

Congressman Lindbergh concentrated on teaching his son to be independent, self-reliant. He took the boy on hunting trips and let him learn to drive when he was eleven. At fourteen Charles drove his mother and an uncle from Little Falls to Los Angeles. With breakdowns, delays, and bad roads, the trip took nearly six weeks.

Because of constant moves from Little Falls to Washington and Detroit, Charles's schooling was helter-skelter. When the United States entered World War I he was given high school credits for working on a farm and was graduated at sixteen. He liked farm work and kept to it for a time. But his father and mother, both college graduates, insisted that Slim (he was now more than six feet tall with not a spare ounce of flesh on him) follow suit.

So in 1920 Slim entered the University of Wisconsin at Madison to study mechanical engineering. He rode his motorcycle from Little Falls to Madison and kept it in his room when he was not racing it or repairing it. In a year or so, alas, his sketchy college preparation caught up with him. He disliked the discipline of study and did poorly at it. In the spring of 1922 he dropped out of school.

At this time Lindbergh had never been up in a plane, had never even been close to one. But he had seen planes in the sky, and he had heard stories of the pleasures and perils of flight. He knew what he wanted to do. He drove his motorcycle to Lincoln, Nebraska, and signed up as a student pilot with the Nebraska Aircraft Corporation. Tuition, paid in advance, was $500.

But the school folded before Lindbergh had been

taught to fly solo. His eight hours of dual-control instruction were scarcely enough. So he tied in with a barnstorming pilot. ("Barnstorming" meant going to county fairs and the like, stunt flying for the crowds and giving rides to all who could pay five dollars for fifteen minutes or so in the air.)

Soon Slim was wing-walking—actually leaving the cockpit and walking out on a wing during flight—and parachuting. After saving enough money, he bought a World War I Jenny with a top speed of 75 miles an hour. On this plane he taught himself to solo. After another barnstorming tour of several states he flew home to give his father his first airplane ride. Lindbergh Senior didn't like it. Slim also gave his mother her first flight. The record says she did like it.

After a time Lindbergh realized that barnstorming was a dead-end venture. So in 1924 he took the entrance exams for the air service. He was accepted and became one of 104 air cadets at Brooks Field, San Antonio, Texas.

In the air Lindbergh was a superb student, easily the best in his class. In the classroom, he was something else at first. But low grades on his first tests helped him make up his mind to hit his textbooks hard. By the time he finished school his test grades were in the 90s. The 104 cadets who started the course were reduced to 18 at graduation. Lindbergh was top man.

Taking his commission in the reserves, Lindbergh hunted for a flying job in civil aviation. He became chief pilot—there were two other fliers—for a company under contract to fly airmail between St. Louis and Chicago, a distance of 285 miles.

The airmail service was a risky enterprise, run on a shoestring. The planes were wartime De Havillands with

Liberty engines. The routes were unmarked and unlighted, and there were no airfields for emergency landings. A pilot in trouble had one flare to drop, and if he was lucky, a cornfield to land in. Nevertheless, Lindbergh and the two pilots under him chalked up a fine record for on-time delivery of the airmail.

Flying the mail, despite occasional forced landings, soon became routine. Lindbergh's mind, as he flew the familiar course, turned to other considerations. Why not fly directly from St. Louis to New York? It could be done in a better plane, the Wright-Bellanca, for example. And why limit the flight to a St. Louis–New York run? The Wright-Bellanca with added gas tanks could go much farther. Why not New York to Paris?

Once in Lindbergh's head, the idea of a New York-to-Paris flight grew swiftly. There was the challenge of the flight itself. No one had yet soloed across the Atlantic; no pilot team had yet flown nonstop for the 3,600 miles that separate New York and Paris.

And there was the Orteig prize of $25,000. That sum would cover all costs, including buying the plane. Beyond the immediate challenge and the prize money Lindbergh did not dare to think.

The plane alone would cost at least $10,000. Lindbergh had saved up about $2,000. Where to get the rest? Lindbergh enlisted several St. Louis businessmen in his cause and set out to buy a Wright-Bellanca. But the Wright people said that the planned flight was too risky; a failure would give the company a bad name. Tony Fokker had opened an aircraft factory in New Jersey after the war; Lindbergh asked to buy a single-seater, single-engine plane. Like the Wright firm, the Fokker company said no —too great a risk.

But the Wright Whirlwind engine was for sale. Now Lindbergh looked for an aircraft manufacturer who would custom-build a plane to house the Wright engine and all the special features Lindbergh wanted for a transatlantic flight.

He found such a company in San Diego, California—the Ryan Airlines. The price, $6,000, was right, and Ryan promised to meet Lindbergh's deadline. (Lindbergh was in a hurry because other fliers were already preparing for a shot at the Orteig prize.)

Lindbergh came to San Diego to work with the Ryan staff. Together they designed and built a plane that would achieve maximum distance. The plane, without an extra ounce of weight in its whole frame, would carry 425 gallons of gasoline. The cockpit was tailored to fit Lindbergh's six feet three inches of height and 170 pounds of weight.

To honor his St. Louis financiers, Lindbergh named the plane *The Spirit of St. Louis*. The name was prominently displayed on the plane's silver-painted fuselage. Lindbergh test-flew the craft in California, then brought it to St. Louis. His backers wanted him to do a little celebrating, but he was eager to be off. He stayed in St. Louis overnight, and the next morning he flew to Curtiss Field in New York.

Waiting for suitable takeoff weather, Lindbergh had to linger in New York for a week. He was dogged by hordes of reporters, all eager for some word about the forthcoming flight that could be featured in the papers.

The public was already fascinated by Lindbergh—boyish-looking, without a big organization behind him, ready to fly the Atlantic alone. People wanted to know more and more about this shy and modest young man. Lindbergh demanded that his privacy be respected, but the newsmen were having none of that. So the cat reporters chased the mouse Lindbergh every time he appeared. They called him "Lucky Lindy" in their news stories.

Rain fell on the evening of May 19, 1927, but the weather bureau predicted a clear sky by morning. That night *The Spirit of St. Louis* was towed to nearby Roosevelt Field, which had a longer runway, and fueled to the brim. Lindbergh left his hotel room early next morning. He had not slept at all, but he was wide awake, eager to get on about his business.

Lindbergh took off at exactly 7:24 A.M. on May 20, 1927. The plane, loaded a little beyond its capacity with fuel, barely cleared the telephone wires at the end of the runway. Lindbergh first flew over Long Island Sound, Connecticut, and Massachusetts, and then he headed out over the open sea. Ahead lay Newfoundland. After he had passed this Canadian island, he would be truly on his own.

At a cruising altitude of 10,000 feet and an average speed of something more than 100 miles an hour, *The Spirit of St. Louis* moved steadily along. As the plane flew eastward, night soon approached, and Lindbergh steered by the stars.

About a third of the way across, Lindbergh's sleeplessness on the previous night caught up with him. From then on in, he fought the battle of sleep, which threatened to put him under every time he relaxed. To keep himself awake he scooped fresh air into his cockpit.

He would not eat his sandwiches for fear that the process of digesting them would bring on sleep. He recited to himself the disasters that falling asleep would cause. Throughout the entire transit he never dozed off for more than a few seconds. Seductive, soothing, death-dealing sleep was his worst enemy.

Somehow Lindbergh managed to make it through the night and into the morning. He flew through cloud banks and contrary winds, changing course when necessary to keep on his charted track. About 27 hours after leaving New York, he saw small fishing boats in the water below. He knew then that continental Europe lay just ahead.

Soon he sighted Ireland and saw people on the beach waving to him. Now wide awake, he piloted his way across Ireland, the south of England, and the English Channel. Reaching France by nightfall, he followed the lighted beacons to Paris. There below him he saw the lovely City of Lights. He managed to locate Le Bourget airport. And he saw, to his alarm, a crowd of thousands waiting for him.

Lindbergh landed, but before he could leave his cockpit the crowd descended on him. Some lifted him to their shoulders and bore him off in triumph. Others—the inevitable souvenir seekers—began ripping pieces of fabric from the plane's wings.

He was finally rescued from the clutches of the crowd and carried away to safety. It was three in the morning be-

Shortly before taking off on his epochal flight from New York to Paris, Charles A. Lindbergh stops for photo near *Spirit of St. Louis.*

fore he was delivered to the American Embassy, where the U.S. ambassador to France, Myron T. Herrick, officially welcomed him. After 63 hours without sleep, Lindbergh was bedded down in the embassy's guest room.

The crowd demonstration at Le Bourget was only a sample of the acclaim that awaited Lindbergh wherever he went. President Calvin Coolidge promoted him from captain to colonel in the air service reserve and sent a cruiser to carry him back to America and its wildly enthusiastic public. Parades, banquets, speeches, medals by the score —all were his in an outpouring of praise never equaled before or since.

Popular songs were written about him. Lapel buttons, cigar bands, and countless mementos bore his name (or his nickname, Lucky Lindy) and his picture. The $25,000 Orteig prize was dwarfed by gifts to Lindbergh valued at an estimated $2,000,000.

Lindbergh turned the gifts over to the Missouri Historical Society. He wrote a book called *We*, which earned him a considerable sum. But he turned down offers worth millions to star in movies, to promote certain products, to lecture, to appear on stage. He did accept a few fees for endorsing products he had actually used in his flight. But he turned down others that would have made him an instant millionaire. These refusals only made him more popular.

The rest of Lindbergh's life was marked by his efforts to escape the limelight. In 1929 he married Anne Morrow, daughter of the U.S. ambassador to Mexico. She became an able flier and acted as his copilot in many pioneering flights to distant places.

In 1932 Charles, Jr., their firstborn child, was kidnapped from their home in Hopewell, New Jersey. The baby's body was found in a shallow grave in the woods about a mile from the Lindbergh home. Soon an unemployed carpenter named Bruno Richard Hauptmann was arrested with some of the ransom money in his possession. He was tried, found guilty, and executed for the crime.

To escape the public attention forced on them by this tragic episode, the Lindberghs went to live in England for several years. Lindbergh worked quietly with aircraft manufacturers to build better planes and to find new air routes.

In the late 1930s Lindbergh became involved in a mistaken effort to keep world peace. He visited Nazi Germany, its leader Adolf Hitler, and its air chief Hermann Göring. He accepted medals from the Nazi government and became convinced that Nazi air power was too strong to be challenged.

Returning to the United States, Lindbergh became one of the spokesmen for the America First movement. He made many speeches arguing that the United States should stay out of Europe's wars. The U.S. government and much of the American public turned against him, and President Roosevelt accepted his resignation as colonel.

When the United States entered World War II in December 1941 Lindbergh spoke no more. He continued his work with aircraft manufacturers, and privately, unofficially, flew combat missions in the Pacific to study the planes in action. After the war he kept on as an aviation consultant. He wrote a new book about his famous flight, called *The Spirit of St. Louis*, in 1953 (see Bibliography).

Lindbergh died at his hideaway home in Hawaii in 1974. To the last he was his own man—honest (sometimes mistakenly so), incorruptible, with a never-shaken faith in the future of flying.

CHAPTER 10
TO AUSTRALIA, THEN AROUND THE WORLD

ROSS SMITH, CHARLES KINGSFORD-SMITH, WILEY POST

One of the most active members of the British Commonwealth, as it was of the old British Empire, is Australia. But this "Down Under" country, astride its own continent in the South Pacific, is many thousands of miles away from Britain. It is nearly that same distance, traveling the other way, from California.

Despite the distance, Australia is distinctively British in many ways. It keeps close ties with Britain. It has the same form of government, the same language. It trades extensively with Britain, and many of its young people attend British universities.

But until the advent of air travel, passengers Britain-bound from Australia spent several weeks aboard ocean liners. It was a long, long voyage. No wonder, then, that pilots right after World War I were eager to try their luck in reaching Australia by air.

If they could do it in days rather than weeks, both Britain and Australia would gain. To encourage fliers to make the long and hazard-filled journey, the Australian government offered a 10,000-pound prize to the first person to make the trip in less than thirty days.

Captain Smith and Crew

THE PRIZEWINNER was a team headed by Captain Ross Smith, just separated from the Australian Flying Corps, a wartime partner of the RAF. Also on the team were Smith's brother Keith as navigator and Jim Bennett and Wally Shiers as mechanics. They too had served in World War I in the air. The Vickers company had furnished them with a Vickers Vimy, just like the one in which Alcock and Brown had recently crossed the Atlantic.

On the morning of November 12, 1919, just a year and a day after the World War I Armistice had been signed, Smith and partners took off from Hounslowe Airdrome near London. Battling ice and fog, the Vimy crew reached their first stop, Lyons, France. After a night's sleep they were off to Pisa, Italy.

Rain grounded them at Pisa for two days, and wind and bad weather chased them across the Apennine Mountains to Crete. The weather improved as they approached Cairo, Egypt, but head winds forced them down in Iraq. Then it was on to Karachi (in India then, now in Pakistan) and to Delhi, India. Soon they were in Burma, then a stop in Bangkok, where the mechanics gave the Vimy's engines a quick overhaul.

Between Bangkok and Darwin, Australia, their destination, there were no real airfields, only a few landing strips hacked out of the jungle or laid down on the desert sands. Even the landing facility at Singapore consisted merely of the straight leg of a racetrack oval.

From there the Smith crewmen were off to Batavia (now Djakarta, Indonesia's capital), then to Surabaja. The Surabaja strip turned out to be swampy, and the Vimy bogged down in the mud. Smith couldn't take off until helpful spectators brought hundreds of bamboo mats to make a runway. Next stop: Bima, and after that, the island of Timor.

Now Smith and company faced a long and hazardous last flight. It was 470 miles from Timor to Darwin, and the Vimy was showing the strain of thousands of miles of continuous flying.

In spite of difficulties, on December 10, 1919, Ross Smith set his plane down at the Darwin airport. The journey had taken twenty-eight of the thirty days allotted, and they won the 10,000-pound prize. It was a great day for the crew and for Australia.

Two Charlies across the Pacific

THE EASTBOUND route between Britain and Australia is largely over land, with only the Timor-Darwin leg over a long stretch of water. But the westward flight from California is virtually an all-water route. An aviator can land on only a few Pacific islands, for repairs and refueling, along the way. Today, commercial and military flight navigators have precise instruments for locating those stops.

But in 1928 flying over the Pacific was a different story. It took great courage and a huge quantity of the daredevil spirit to win success in aviation's early days. Charles

Kingsford-Smith and his copilot Charles Ulm had plenty of both. They were the first to fly from California to Australia —from San Francisco to Brisbane—a distance of about 8,000 miles. Using a trimotor Fokker, the *Southern Cross*, they made it in five air days.

Kingsford-Smith was an RAF pilot in World War I, an ace with five downed enemy planes to his credit. After the war he tried a number of aviation ventures and failed in just about all of them.

He applied for entry in the 1919 England-to-Australia competition, but was turned down because he had no real plan for refueling along the way. He set up an aerial sightseeing business in England, but that failed after one summer. He flew stunts for movie cameramen in Hollywood, California. He cropdusted rice fields in northern California. He flew for a small Australian outfit, Digger Airways. There often seemed to be something shady about Kingsford-Smith's enterprises.

Charles Ulm had promotional ability as well as flying skills. He entered the picture when he sold the Sydney (Australia) *Sun* on the idea of making air photos of the arrival of a British naval fleet at Sydney Harbor. The resulting front-page photo splash was spectacular and earned Ulm the friendship and later the backing of the Sydney *Sun*.

Ulm and Kingsford-Smith met and were soon talking about a transpacific aerial journey. To win a name for themselves—and to enlist the aid of financial backers— they organized a flight around the perimeter of the Australian continent, a distance of about 7,500 miles. They made it in ten days, five and one half hours. (Flying 750 miles a day for ten days was a real feat in the 1920s.)

The around-the-continent flight produced generous promises of aid, including some government help, for a transpacific transit. Kingsford-Smith and Ulm came to the United States in search of a plane for that flight. The search proved unexpectedly long and difficult, and backers retracted their pledges. The plane they finally located was slipping away.

Out of the blue the two met G. Allan Hancock, a wealthy steamship owner. Hancock took Kingsford-Smith and Ulm on a cruise to Mexico. On the way he told them that he would buy the plane and lend it to them for the crossing.

The plane problem solved, Kingsford-Smith and Ulm hired Harry Lyons, a Maine ship's captain, as navigator. They put James Warner, a Kansas City radioman, in charge of communications. And they ordered a name painted on the Fokker's fuselage: *Southern Cross*, the constellation that guides sailors and fliers in the Southern Hemisphere.

On the morning of May 31, 1928, the *Southern Cross* took off from the Oakland (California) Airport, Hawaii-bound. It took 27½ hours to cover the 2,400 miles to Wheeler Field, near Honolulu. The only trouble the crew encountered was a temporary deafness induced by the roar of the three Wright Whirlwind engines.

Next day the *Southern Cross* was ferried over to a beach on the island of Kauai. The beach offered a 4,500-foot runway. This whole length was needed because the *Southern Cross* was taking off with full gasoline tanks.

The tanks had to be brim-full because the next stop was at Suva in the Fiji Islands, 3,200 miles away. Even if Harry Lyons, the navigator, led the *Southern Cross* di-

Charles Kingsford-Smith (right), first to fly from California to Australia, leaves plane after landing on airstrip in northern Australia.

rectly to Suva, there would be gasoline for only another 600 miles in the tanks. And Suva, with an area of 60 by 90 miles, was really only a pinpoint in the vast Pacific.

The *Southern Cross* took off early on the morning of June 4. Kingsford-Smith and Ulm took turns piloting, keeping the altitude low to save on fuel. They ran into rain and storm clouds and had to fly higher to avoid them. They worried about fuel consumption, engine trouble, and their precise location in the sky. And when they finally sighted Suva, they feared that the makeshift landing strip, 1,300 feet long and surrounded by trees and fences, was too short.

Their worries were groundless. The *Southern Cross* made a safe landing, a little gasoline still in its tanks, its engines in good condition. The crew stayed on Suva for two days, resting, refueling, and joining in the celebration of the first plane landing in the Fiji Islands.

On June 8 the *Southern Cross* started for Brisbane, Australia, 2,200 miles away. Almost at once it ran into a torrential rainstorm that pitched and tossed the plane for at least four hours, throwing it badly off course. It was a truly frightening experience for the crew.

Gradually the sky cleared, and the navigator guided the *Southern Cross* back on course. Huge crowds at Brisbane made Kingsford-Smith and his men forget (at least temporarily) their recent peril. They were able to enjoy their triumph—the first successful flight from California to Australia.

Around the World

IN THE late 1920s the public became fascinated by the German-built rigid airships called *dirigibles*. These were lighter-than-air vessels carried into the sky by bags of hydrogen held in a huge elongated "envelope." Crew, passengers, and engines were housed in compartments attached to the hull of the envelope.

A dirigible could reach a speed of 70 miles an hour, carry dozens of passengers and crew, and could stay aloft as long as its food and water held out. In 1929 the *Graf Zeppelin* circled the world in twenty-one days, making only four stops along the way.

The record gave airplane pilots something to shoot at. They knew, of course, that they could fly faster than 70 miles an hour. But could a plane of that era hold up for a trip around the planet? Breaking the *Graf Zeppelin's* record meant that there could be no long halts for engine overhaul or replacement of major parts. There had to be a minimum of fuel stops and a maximum of time in the air.

The *Graf Zeppelin's* record was a challenge. In 1931 a man named Wiley Post accepted that challenge. With his navigator, Harold Gatty, he circled the world in eight days, 15 hours, 51 minutes. He broke the dirigible record by more than twelve days.

A Texan by birth, Wiley Post grew up in Oklahoma. Machinery always interested young Wiley, but books did not. He dropped out of school after finishing the eighth grade. At nineteen he became an oil-field worker in his state's booming oil industry. Then he took his first ride in a plane, and he was hooked forever after.

How to get a job connected with flying? When Post was twenty-six he found a way. A barnstorming crew was performing in a nearby town, and Post heard that its parachute jumper had been grounded by an injury. Although he had never parachuted before, he passed the jump test and was hired.

Post stayed with the barnstormers for two years. But the public gradually lost interest in aerial acrobatics. Post went back to an oil field, still wanting to be a flier. He planned to save money and buy his own plane.

The day Post started work in the oil field was a black day for him. Nearby, another worker was pounding an iron bolt with a sledgehammer. An iron fragment shot into Post's left eye, affecting vision in both eyes. Surgeons had to remove the left one, but the right eye gradually returned to normal. With one eye missing, Post at first couldn't tell whether one object was smaller than another or simply farther away. Months of practice restored his skill at judging sizes and distances.

Workmen's Compensation awarded Post the sum of $1,800 for his injury. He bought a plane and began earning money by piloting oil men around, teaching student fliers, and barnstorming on weekends.

Post soon got married and then needed more money. He became the personal pilot for F. C. Hall, a rich Oklahoma oil man. Hall's plane was a four-seater Lockheed Vega with an enclosed cabin. It was called the *Winnie Mae*, after Hall's daughter. When Hall did not need the *Winnie Mae* for business trips, Post was free to use it as he wished.

The oil business dipped, and Hall needed cash. He sold the *Winnie Mae* and let Post go. Post got a job with Lockheed and learned much about aircraft design. In time Hall's business improved and he rehired Post. He told Post to buy a new Vega (calling the new one *Winnie Mae* as well). He also promised to let Post make some of those long-distance flights he'd been planning.

The new *Winnie Mae* had all of the latest features. A monoplane, it was equipped with a 420-horsepower Pratt

& Whitney Wasp engine. Cruising speed was 150 miles an hour, top speed 190 miles an hour.

In it Post won the Men's Air Derby in the 1930 National Air Races. The event was a Los Angeles–Chicago nonstop flight for planes that could carry at least 1,000 pounds as payload. Hall was pleased with the win. He allowed Post to keep the prize of $7,500 and encouraged him to make more record-breaking flights.

Post had already decided that he wanted to fly around the world. Preparations began at once. As navigator he hired Harold Gatty, experienced at charting courses at sea and in the air. He made Gatty responsible for the route, for getting permission to land in countries along the route, and for stocking refueling stations with the vitally needed aviation gasoline. Post took the responsibility for seeing that Lockheed improved the plane's distance performance.

Pilot and navigator flew the *Winnie Mae* to Roosevelt Field on Long Island, New York, and settled down to await good flying weather. They waited one day short of a month. On June 22, 1931, at 4:55 A.M. they took off for Newfoundland. The *Winnie Mae* put down on that Atlantic outpost after a seven hour flight. Less than four hours later, Post and Gatty were off for England.

Fog and storm over the Atlantic prevented Gatty from taking star sights, so they flew by instruments. They landed at an RAF field near Liverpool, stopping only to lunch and refuel. On to Hanover, Germany, then to Berlin. There they were wined and dined and put up for a night's refreshing slumber.

Next stop: Moscow, a thousand miles ahead. A bucketing rain all along the course made Post and Gatty feel as though they were flying through Niagara Falls. They made Moscow by nightfall.

The *Winnie Mae* was refueled during the night, but Post forgot to specify U.S. gallons. So the tanks were overfilled with imperial gallons, 20 percent larger than the American variety. Result: the *Winnie Mae* was too heavy for takeoff. They had to wait three hours while the extra gasoline was pumped out.

The trip across the vast expanse of the Soviet Union had just begun. They made Novosibirsk, in Russia's interior, in good time, spending the night there. A refueling stop in Irkutsk, then on to Blagoveshchensk in Siberia.

There they ran into real trouble. Two inches of water covered the airfield, turning it into a sea of mud. The *Winnie Mae*'s wheels sank and then settled down as if rooted there. It took fourteen hours to pull the plane free.

The *Winnie Mae* was still in the Soviet Union as it approached Khabarovsk, last stop in Siberia. From there the plane winged on to Alaska, touching down on the beach near Solomon, a native village. Trying to take off from the beach, the *Winnie Mae*'s wheels foundered in the sand and the propeller tips bent. Handyman Post pounded the tips back into position.

At Fairbanks, Alaska, the exhausted fliers napped for three hours while the plane was refueled and a new propeller put on. Then they flew south to Edmonton, Canada. There trouble found them again.

As in Blagoveshchensk, the airfield was covered with water. This time Post managed to keep the *Winnie Mae* from being mired in the mud while landing. But how could they take off from this surface? A Canadian airmail pilot provided the answer. Why not take off from Portage Avenue, the two-mile-long paved street that runs between airfield and town?

At once the electric cables were removed from posts

along the street, and the street itself was cleared of every obstacle. Yet there was no room for slides or slips. Fearful but calm, Post rolled the *Winnie Mae* down the street and made a perfect takeoff. Late that afternoon, plane and crew made it to Cleveland's Municipal Airport. Refueled, they were off to New York to complete their circle of the globe.

Enthusiastic New Yorkers welcomed Post and Gatty with parades and celebrations that lasted for days. They acclaimed the two as heroes, and they meant it—for the moment. Gatty bowed out and returned to his school for aerial navigators. Post began work on a long-cherished dream: to set up the Wiley Post Institute for Aeronautical Research.

But Post found few backers. The Great Depression of the 1930s had set in, and money was scarce. There was another reason as well. Many people thought that Post, with only a grade-school education, had no business wanting to be the head of a research foundation. They also believed that Gatty had been the real planner of the flight and that Post had been only an aerial chauffeur.

Neither of these charges was valid. But Post felt he had to show the world his real worth. There was only one way to do it, he thought: circle the globe again—by himself.

Surprisingly, Post found enough backers for this project. He talked the Sperry Gyroscope Company into installing an experimental autopilot in the *Winnie Mae*. This was a device that monitored the instrument panel by itself. And the U.S. Army lent him a new direction finder. These two instruments would help make up for the loss of navigator Gatty.

With the *Winnie Mae* completely overhauled, Post took off from New York for Berlin on July 15, 1933. En route, trouble developed in the autopilot, and mechanics in Berlin tried to fix it. The trouble persisted on his way to Novosibirsk, Russia, and a new problem showed up: in Berlin he had forgotten his maps of Russia. So he had to stop in East Prussia for maps. He also made unscheduled stops in Moscow and Irkutsk for more repairs to the autopilot. Nevertheless he was in Khabarovsk, in Siberia, ahead of schedule.

Crossing over from Siberia to Alaska was perilous. Post's radio and direction finder quit, and he became lost in the overcast. He finally made it to the mining town of Flat. But in landing on the little airstrip his landing gear crumpled and his propeller became bent. Luckily, help was available from Fairbanks, 300 miles away. The *Winnie Mae* was repaired during the night, and Post was again on his way.

Refueling in Edmonton, Canada, he took off for New York. More than 50,000 excited well-wishers loudly cheered his arrival on the night of July 22. Post had earned their cheers. He had circled the world—alone—in exactly 7 days, 18 hours, 49½ minutes, more than 21 hours faster than his first flight.

In 1935 Post came to a tragic end. On a trip to Alaska with Will Rogers, the famous humorist, his plane plunged into a lake, and the two were drowned. The whole world mourned the noted flier and the beloved comedian, but Oklahoma people were perhaps the saddest of all. Both Post and Rogers had come from their state.

CHAPTER **11**
THE BATTLE OF BRITAIN

DOUGLAS BADER

The six-year global struggle that history records as World War II began in September 1939. Nazi German forces under dictator Adolf Hitler invaded Poland, bent on conquest. France and Britain sternly demanded that Hitler withdraw his troops. Hitler refused. The two protesting nations, acting under a mutual defense treaty with Poland, declared war on Germany. The Nazi cauldron of aggressions had been seething for years. Now it boiled over.

Germany, Italy, and Japan—soon to be called the Axis—had been marching in and taking over foreign territories, whole pieces of nations, ever since 1931. Germany was the grossest offender in these seizures (although Japan was not far behind). The Germans piously pleaded that they were only seeking *lebensraum* (living space) for their nation's expanding population. To keep an uneasy peace, France and Britain, leaders of the Western European nations, had gone along with these territorial takeovers.

In September 1938 these leaders had agreed to let Germany annex a part of Czechoslovakia after Hitler vowed that this would be his last demand. But in March 1939 Hitler broke his promise and seized all of Czechoslovakia. It was then that France and Britain abandoned their policy of appeasement and signed the treaty with Poland.

The Nazi invasion of Poland was a *blitzkrieg*, a lightning war. The German Luftwaffe (air force) knocked out all Polish air bases. The German panzer (armored and mechanized) divisions closed in on Polish troops. Within a couple of weeks the Soviet Union, at the time an ally of Germany, also invaded Poland. The two soon divided the conquered land between themselves.

For months after the conquest of Poland, there was little fighting. The French settled down behind their Maginot Line, the Germans behind their Siegfried Line, each waiting for the other to advance. The British set up blockades just outside German harbors, hoping to halt deliveries of cargoes, but the blockades were ineffective.

Germany was just taking a breather, biding its time, regrouping its forces. It started moving again in April 1940 by overrunning Denmark and Norway. In May, Belgium, the Netherlands, and Luxembourg were added to the tally of Nazi conquests. In June France fell. Britain was to be next.

Hitler was already planning his Operation Sea Lion—an invasion of the island nation of Britain after the Luftwaffe had demolished British defenses. Then the Nazi ground forces would come ashore along the English Channel and North Sea beaches. They would march in and take control.

Operation Sea Lion was scheduled for the early fall of 1940. It never took place. The projected German air blitz was stopped cold by the skill and courage of British airmen in the now-famous Battle of Britain.

In July of 1940 Hitler had issued his Directive No. 16, which began: "As England, in spite of the hopelessness of her military position, has so far not shown herself willing to come to any compromise, I have decided to begin to prepare for, and if necessary to carry out, an invasion of England.

"This operation is dictated by the necessity of eliminating Great Britain as a base from which the war against Germany can be fought, and if necessary the island will be occupied. . . ."

With these grim words the machinery designed to wipe out Britain began rumbling. August 13 was chosen as *Adler Tag* (Eagle Day), the day when thousands of Nazi planes would darken the skies over Britain and bomb it into submission. There was no secret about the planned onslaught. All Britain knew just about when it was scheduled to take place. The British people were ready.

Their defense preparations were strengthened by the heartening words of their prime minister, Winston Churchill: "The whole fury and might of the enemy must soon be turned on us. Hitler knows that he will have to break us on this island or lose the war. If we can stand up to him, all Europe may be free and the life of the world may move forward. . . . But if we fail, then the whole world . . . will sink into the abyss of a new Dark Age. . . .

"Let us therefore brace ourselves to our duties, and so bear ourselves that, if the British Empire and Commonwealth last for a thousand years, men will still say, 'This was their finest hour.'"

To defend itself, Britain had sixty air squadrons, with a total of 704 planes ready for combat, plus 289 in reserve.

About two-thirds were Hurricane and Spitfire fighters. The rest were Bristol Blenheims, light bombers used as fighters, and Boulton Paul Defiant two-seater fighters. In all, there were 1,253 pilots to man these craft.

Long before Eagle Day was to take place, German bombers and fighters began probing for targets along the English Channel coast. British fighters rose to meet them, and the result was usually a standoff. The Nazis eventually retreated, with one or more planes lost, but they took an equal toll from the British.

Eagle Day finally arrived. The Nazis attacked in force from the air, but their tactics were uncertain. They waffled and wavered and succeeded in bombing only a few airfields. They lost forty-five aircraft to Britain's thirteen. And if this first day's strike was any indication, the Germans were beginning to lose the Battle of Britain.

Legless Legend

TYPICAL OF the British airmen who routed the Nazi foe was Douglas Bader. In another sense, however, he was not typical at all. For Douglas Bader had a severely crippling physical handicap.

Doug Bader should never have been allowed in the air. At least, that's what a great many people thought. After all, a man whose legs had both been amputated couldn't fly with artificial ones. Or could he? In the Battle of Britain, Douglas Bader proved that a man fighting for his country is capable of great achievement, legs or no legs.

Bader learned to fly at Cranwell, the RAF's school for flying officers. From boyhood he had been a superb athlete, excelling at every major sport. He became an equally superb fighter pilot. But Bader was also a crazy daredevil, who took all kinds of flying chances forbidden by the RAF.

In 1931 friends challenged Bader, then only twenty-one, to take one of those chances. Bader accepted the dare. He did a series of stunts, then, at low level, threw his plane into a tight turn. The wingtip brushed the ground and pulled the plane down. It rolled over and over and finally collapsed into a tangled jumble.

Bader was knocked out briefly. When he came to, he found himself sitting on his left leg, his right foot jammed into a corner of the cockpit. He was rushed to the hospital in a semi-coma. The surgeons operated immediately. They amputated the right leg above the knee, the left leg six inches below the knee.

The early stages of recovery were an ordeal. Bader lay in agony, his mind wandering, not really knowing what had happened to his body. But when he heard people around him whispering that he was dying, he began to fight back. He was still alive; he was determined to remain so. Gradually he realized that his legs were gone. He made up his mind to live, and live actively, as he was.

For a time he got along on crutches and one wooden leg. When the stumps healed, he was fitted for artificial legs. With these strapped into place, he swore he'd never use a cane or crutch again—and he never did.

Getting about on artificial legs was a torment at first. He simply did not know how to control them. In time he learned. The right leg remained less controllable than the left, so he had the foot pedals on his car adjusted to work off the left foot.

Bader learned to fly again and passed all the tests. However, the RAF banned him from flying and seated him behind a desk. The 1930s were years of retreat along many fronts. In 1933 the RAF retired Bader for ill health.

At twenty-three Bader was not ready to retire. He got

a job with an international oil company and married a woman named Thelma. She soothed his rebellious spirit and played golf, tennis, and squash with him. (Despite the amputations Bader was amazingly skilled at these and other sports.) They even went dancing together.

When war clouds gathered in the late 1930s, Bader wrote the RAF many times, pleading to be allowed back in the air. A few weeks after the war started in September 1939 he was called in, examined, and found fit for flight duty. This was a complete turnabout from his 1933 dismissal.

Always feisty, Bader argued with his superiors over flight tactics. He didn't like flying in set formations. He preferred to scramble into dogfights, catching the enemy by surprise and tricky maneuvering.

Despite his argumentative nature (or perhaps because of it) he was promoted to flight lieutenant of No. 222 Squadron. Flying a Hurricane, he taught his pilots how to fire and avoid counterfire.

No. 222 Squadron saw no real action until the end of May and the start of June 1940, when Dunkirk was evacuated. This town on the channel coast of France was the temporary refuge for hundreds of thousands of British troops retreating after France fell to the Nazis. The troops were met by a ragtag armada of hundreds of British naval vessels, plus fishing and ferry boats, private yachts, anything that floated. Under air cover they took aboard the whole fleeing army and sailed it safely back to England.

Bader's No. 222 Squadron helped provide this air cover. They kept the Nazis at bay and made sure that Britain's army would live to fight another day. Bader had the personal satisfaction of knocking at least one Messerschmitt out of the sky.

Right after Dunkirk, Bader was appointed squadron leader of No. 242 Squadron. This was a Canadian outfit that had fought in France until it fled to avoid being trapped by the conquering Nazis. It had taken a beating, and its wounds were visible. The men were demoralized. They showed it by being wild, defiant, unwilling to be ordered around.

Baden faced the group briefly at their airfield. He quickly assumed that the squadron distrusted him because of his artificial legs. At once he climbed into the cockpit of a waiting Hurricane and demonstrated his prowess in the air. He put the plane through loops, rolls, spins, all sorts of aerial acrobatics. Landing, he left the field without a word.

Next morning he scolded the men for their sloppy personal appearance. He was promptly told that they had been forced to leave their French airfield in a hurry and had no clothes but what they were wearing. They had retreated from field to field in France, begging gasoline and food, going up time after time, but always being beaten back.

Now they were in England with no spare parts for their planes, no maintenance gear, no extra clothes. In retreating they had lost nearly half the men in the squadron.

Bader apologized and promised to replace their losses in men and equipment. With that, he and the Canadians became great friends. He taught them how to fly under his command. When the Battle of Britain started, No. 242 Squadron was prepared. But days passed before it was called into action. Bader sweated and fretted over the delay.

The call came on August 30. The North Weald fighter station was under attack. Bader's group of nine Hurricanes scrambled to meet an oncoming assemblage of perhaps a hundred enemy bombers and fighters. Led by Bader, the Canadians tore right into the foe, swooping, turning, diving, climbing, and firing every time they saw a Nazi in their gunsights.

The score: twelve confirmed German kills, several more planes damaged. The enemy was routed and sent fleeing home. And not a bullet hole in any of the Hurricanes, not a bomb dropped on North Weald.

That same night Bader asked his chief for two more squadrons to fly under his command. The more planes he had, the more enemies would be shot down, he asserted. His chief consented. Next day Bader led three squadrons, destroying twenty Dornier bombers and Messerschmitt fighters. The British lost four Hurricanes and two pilots.

Thereafter Bader led five squadrons, totalling sixty fighters. His unit was called the 12 Group Wing. On one of the biggest days of the Battle of Britain, September 15, they scored fifty-two kills, eight more probables. On September 18 they shot down thirty enemy planes, plus six probables. On neither day did Bader's wing suffer any losses.

For his valor in the Battle of Britain, Bader was awarded the Distinguished Service Order and the Distinguished Flying Cross. In March of 1941 he was transferred to the Tangmere air base to command three squadrons of Spitfires. Their assignment was to escort bomber groups as they struck enemy factories and rail junctions on the continent.

This was dangerous duty, but Bader flew as though he were going to live forever, never to be hit by enemy fire from the air or ground. His superiors worried that his luck would soon run out and wanted him to take an extended leave. He finally agreed to go at the end of August.

Bader's luck did run out on August 9, 1941. His squadron tangled with a dozen Messerschmitts over the French coast. Bader saw three of them just ahead and decided to go after them himself. In the ensuing dogfight Bader's Spitfire ran right into a Messerschmitt. The rear half of the Spitfire was torn away. Bader fell thousands of feet before he was able to wiggle out of his cockpit. Doing so, he left one of his artificial legs behind. Bader parachuted to earth with one leg, an artificial one at that.

His German captors, knowing his reputation, treated him with respect. They asked the British to drop a replacement leg behind their lines, which was done. Bader did not settle down to become a "good" prisoner. He tried to escape time after time and was finally locked up in the maximum-security Colditz Castle. He was released by the conquering American 1st Army just after Germany fell in 1945.

Still alive, Bader has become a legend, his name remembered and his story told wherever flying buffs gather.

CHAPTER
DOOLITTLE'S RAIDERS AND BOYINGTON'S BLACK SHEEP

It was Sunday, December 7, 1941. Most Americans were engaged in one or another of their leisurely Sabbath occupations—coming home from church, reading the papers, walking the dog, preparing Sunday dinner. Many radios were turned on, but listened to with only half an ear.

Suddenly the announcer broke in with an attention-riveting bulletin: "The Japanese air force has bombed Pearl Harbor in Hawaii! Caught completely by surprise, the United States has suffered huge losses in ships, planes, and men. It looks as though America is in World War II at last. More later—stay tuned."

The announcer was right. After twenty-seven months of an uneasy neutrality, the United States was plunged into the firepit of war on two fronts. Just a few hours after the attack, Japan's Emperor Hirohito imperiously proclaimed: "We, by grace of Heaven, Emperor of Japan, seated on the throne of a line unbroken for ages eternal, enjoin upon you, our loyal and brave subjects: We hereby declare war on the United States of America and the British Empire."

America was quick to respond. Next day Congress met to hear President Roosevelt brand December 7 as "a day that will live in infamy" and ask for a declaration of war against Japan. The Senate responded unanimously; the House of Representatives replied with only a single dissenting vote. Soon after, the United States declared war on Germany as well.

The carnage at Pearl Harbor was immense. Dozens of ships at anchor or moored to the docks were sunk or seriously damaged. Hundreds of aircraft caught on the ground were destroyed. Thousands of men, army as well as navy, were killed, missing in action, or badly wounded.

The Japanese had thought they would wipe out America's entire Pacific Fleet in this one massive attack. They were wrong. The fleet had been badly crippled. But it was still alive and soon ready to fight back. So was the army, especially the U.S. Army Air Corps (soon to be renamed the U.S. Army Air Force).

During the weeks after Pearl Harbor, President Roosevelt and his top generals and admirals searched for a way to hit back at Japan immediately. What was needed, they decided, was a bold air bombing strike against industrial targets in Japanese cities. Japan had to be convinced that it could be hurt badly, that it had taken on a foe who would someday win the war. In the same way, Americans had to be convinced that they could rise from the ashes of Pearl Harbor and carry the war right to the enemy's homeland.

But how? America's relations with its new allies, China and Russia, were not strong enough to ask a great favor. That favor would be to furnish an air base from which an air offensive against Japan could be mounted. Nor could U.S. aircraft carriers at that time sail close enough to Japan to launch an air attack—not without great risk to the carrier planes and the carriers themselves.

One man came up with a daring idea. Why not launch a group of long-range army bombers from a carrier? The carrier could keep its distance from patrol planes based in Japan. The bombers could fly their mission over Japan and still have enough fuel to carry them to a safe landing somewhere along China's or Russia's Pacific coasts.

Jimmy Doolittle and Company

AIR CORPS and navy experts studied the proposal and found it workable. The North American B-25 was to be the plane, they decided, and the man they wanted to lead the flight was James H. Doolittle, a lieutenant colonel on the staff of the air corps commanding general.

Jimmy Doolittle, at forty-five, was the ideal man for the job. He was a topnotch flier, knew airplanes inside out, and accepted all challenges, especially risky ones. He had enlisted in 1917 and had served in the air service until 1930. Then he won a Doctor of Science degree from the Massachusetts Institute of Technology and worked for the aviation department of a major oil company. He was recalled to active duty in 1940.

Told of his appointment, Doolittle sped into action. There were a dozen problems to be solved at once. Pilots and crews had to be selected and trained. The B-25s had to be modified to take on a maximum fuel and bomb load. Practice takeoffs had to be made from a field no longer than a carrier's flight deck. No B-25 had ever taken off from so short a runway before. The carrier that was to take Doolittle's Raiders to the scene of action had to be chosen.

Selected for training were twenty-four crews of five men each: pilot, copilot, navigator-gunner, bombardier, engineer-gunner. Eventually sixteen crews would make the flight. They were all volunteers, and each had had experience in flying B-25s. The crews reported in at Eglin Field, Florida, for special training on March 1, 1942.

Doolittle introduced himself to them: "My name is Doolittle. I've been put in charge of the project you men have volunteered for. It's a tough one, and it will be the most dangerous thing any of you have ever been on. Any man can drop out, and nothing will ever be said about it." But details about the project, especially the final destination of the bombers, remained secret.

The crews found the once-familiar B-25s greatly altered. Extra fuel tanks had been installed. The large radios had been removed. So had the belly turret and tail guns. Even the highly secret Norden bombsight had been taken out and a cheaper one installed, one that was actually better for low-level bombing. Each plane was to carry four 500-pound bombs.

Pilots practiced short-run takeoffs as if they were flying off a carrier deck. Bombardiers directed make-believe bombing runs over nearby Florida communities. Engineers fine-tuned their engines and carburetors to save as much fuel as possible. They would need every last drop to reach safety.

The carrier that was to take them within several hundred miles of Tokyo was the *Hornet*, commanded by Captain Marc Mitscher. The *Hornet* was waiting at Alameda Naval Air Station in California on April 1 to take the sixteen B-25s aboard. Loaded, the carrier steamed out to sea, flanked by three cruisers, four destroyers, and a tanker.

That afternoon Captain Mitscher announced over the

ship's speaker: "Now hear this: This force is bound for Tokyo!" It was the first word that the bomber crews had of their destination. And, of course, it was news to the crews of the *Hornet* and its sister ships.

Unknown to Doolittle was the fact that permission to land after the bombing raid had not been cleared with either Russia or China. Russia, still at peace with Japan, wanted no part of any U.S. strike against that country. The Chinese leader, Generalissimo Chiang Kai-shek, did not want the Americans to land anywhere near Japanese-held territory on the Chinese mainland. He feared that an American attack on Japan would bring further Japanese attacks on China. Chiang's fears, unfortunately, turned out to be true.

On April 13 the *Hornet* and its group were joined by the carrier *Enterprise*, plus two cruisers, four destroyers, and a tanker. Aboard the *Enterprise* was Admiral William Halsey, in overall command of this newly formed Task Force 16. The destroyers and tankers dropped out on April 17, but the rest of the task force kept on course.

Early the next morning the U.S. ships were spotted by a Japanese picket vessel. The picket flashed the word to Tokyo. It was time for Doolittle and his men to take action.

At 8 A.M. on April 18 Admiral Halsey sent this message to the *Hornet*: "Launch planes. To Colonel Doolittle and his gallant command: Good luck and God bless you."

With Doolittle's plane in the lead, the sixteen B-25s took off one by one from the *Hornet*'s flight deck. Tokyo was about 600 miles to the north. The flight reached it about twelve noon. Hovering low over their targets, the B-25s released their bombs.

The American raid stunned the people of Tokyo. The

bombardiers had been coached to aim their bombs only at factories, oil refineries, railroad yards, and the like, but they could not help hitting some houses. They did miss hitting Emperor Hirohito's palace, but not by very much.

The total damage caused by the raid was actually small, but the psychological effect was great. Ever since Japan had begun its campaign of conquest in 1931, the people of Japan felt secure in their home islands. Now that feeling of security was gone. Doolittle and his men had proved that Japan could be hit—and hit hard.

After the bombing, the Doolittle flight was by no means out of danger. Fuel was running low. Ahead lay unknown country. Where were the planes—or the men in parachutes—going to land? Would the people be friendly or hostile? How would the Americans find their way to safety?

Doolittle himself was the first to find answers to some of these questions. It was already night, and they were flying over uncharted territory when his B-25 began to fail. He decided that it would be safer to parachute at once than to wait until the plane began to go down.

The crew peeled out of the open hatch. Doolittle was the last to leap. He jumped into the darkness hoping for a soft landing. The terrain was not exactly what he had been counting on. He came down into a rice paddy fertilized by human waste.

Crawling clear, Doolittle found a house with its door locked. He knocked and repeated a Chinese phrase, "Lu-shu hoo megwa fugi," which was supposed to mean "I am an American." The householders apparently did not understand him; at any rate, they did not let him in. He finally crept inside an old mill. It was too cold to fall asleep.

Next morning a farmer led him to a Chinese army post, where a major (who spoke some English) listened to his story. The officer found Doolittle's tale hard to believe. Doolittle tried to prove his claims. He took the major back to the house where he had attempted to gain entry the night before. The people swore he had never been there. He took the major and his men to the rice paddy where he had left his parachute. The chute was gone.

The major became even more hostile. Just then two of his men came out of the house with the parachute. The farm family had hidden it away and denied Doolittle's claim of knocking on their door the night before.

Finally believing Doolittle's story, the major became his friend. He sent soldiers to find the rest of Doolittle's crew, fed Doolittle well, and helped him on his way. The crew members were reunited, each with his story of adventure to tell. None had been hurt, except for cuts and bruises.

Jimmy Doolittle (center), flight crew, and three Chinese friends, rest easy after successful Tokyo bombing in April, 1942.

With his engineer-gunner, Sergeant Paul Leonard, Doolittle located the peak where their empty plane had crashed. The wrecked B-25 was only a jumble of bits and pieces. Despondent, Doolittle felt that he had failed.

True, his flight had actually bombed Tokyo. But now the crews of all his planes except his own were scattered and lost. "Are any of them still alive?" Doolittle kept asking himself.

Leonard attempted to cheer him up. Doolittle, he predicted, would win swift promotion to general as a result of the Tokyo raid. Moreover, he would be awarded the nation's highest honor, the Congressional Medal of Honor. Leonard's predictions came true. Doolittle became a brigadier general and was presented with the coveted medal.

What was even more satisfying to Doolittle was that most of the crew members lived and eventually made it to safety. Only one B-25 was able to land in one piece. This plane put down at a field about forty miles from Vladivostok on the Pacific coast of Russia. Russians seized the plane and confined the crew. They were able to bribe their way free about a year later.

Ten other crews besides Doolittle's parachuted after abandoning their planes. Only one of these crewmen died of injuries sustained in the jump. The other four crews crash-landed. In these landings several crewmen died outright or were badly hurt.

Eight more of those who crashed were captured by the Japanese. A military court sentenced all eight to death. Three were actually executed. The other five were sent to prison for life as "war criminals." One of these died of illness and mistreatment in his cell. The remaining four, after forty months of solitary confinement, were rescued by American forces on August 20, 1945.

The Japanese rage over the Doolittle raid was not confined to the captured fliers. Japanese troops invaded more Chinese territory and turned 20,000 square miles into a wasteland. They forced the Chinese to dig trenches through every airfield and landing strip. They wiped out all villages which had given any sort of help to the downed B-25 crewmen. In all they slaughtered a quarter of a million people in revenge for the raid.

Pappy Boyington and His Black Sheep

EVEN BEFORE Doolittle's daredevil raid on Tokyo, there were American fliers fighting in the Far East. They were there, in fact, long before Pearl Harbor. The American Volunteer Group (AVG) had been flying and fighting for the Chinese since the late 1930s.

In 1941, just weeks before Pearl Harbor, their ranks grew with the addition of 90 pilots and 150 ground crew. They had come to Asia either for money or glory, or both. The engine cowlings of their Curtiss P-40s were painted with a shark's mouth design; hence the name Flying Tigers —"tigers" being short for "tiger sharks."

Among these volunteers was Gregory Boyington, an ex-marine pilot who was barely outdistancing a pursuing posse of bill collectors. His story of action with the Flying Tigers and later with the Marines in the Pacific lit up the nation's TV screens in the 1970s.

Boyington was twenty-eight years old in 1941, a first lieutenant in the Marine Corps. He had been flying for six years, mainly in fighter planes. He was an instructor at the naval air station in Pensacola, Florida, when he was sounded out about joining the Flying Tigers in China.

The marine pilot had heard of the Flying Tigers and

their chief, General Claire Chennault, formerly a captain in the army air corps. He liked what the outfit offered: a chance for adventure, a chance for action in a war that seemed to be bypassing the United States.

The pay offered was good (for those times): $675 a month, plus a bonus of $500 for every Japanese plane knocked out of the sky. In China Boyington's creditors would be far away. And he would be with people who would not criticize his hard drinking. Boyington was a "macho man" long before that phrase entered the English language.

So Boyington resigned from the marines (with the proviso that he could rejoin if the United States entered the war) and drove cross-country to San Francisco. He embarked on a Dutch ship bound for Rangoon, Burma. From there he moved up to Toungoo, in central Burma. Here he met, and was tremendously impressed by, General Chennault. He was not so impressed by Chennault's aides, either Chinese or American, or by the fact that no spare parts were on hand for the P-40s.

It was in the middle of the night, and the AVG pilots were asleep, when they got the word about Pearl Harbor. Fearful of a Japanese attack on their unprotected Toungoo field, the whole group retreated to safer headquarters at Kunming, China. Boyington's squadron saw no action at Kunming. He was relieved when he was sent back to Rangoon to work with Royal Air Force units stationed there.

One day in February 1942 Boyington and nine other Flying Tigers were ordered into the sky to engage several dozen "bandits"—Japanese fighters. From this first encounter with the enemy Boyington barely escaped with his life. He learned one important lesson: never underestimate a Japanese fighter pilot.

Indeed, the Japanese air forces attacking Rangoon grew stronger and stronger. The P-40 pilots were beaten back to Kunming, and the RAF men retreated to India, then a British possession. All along the retreat the Tigers fought pitched battles with the Japanese. They lost many pilots, killed or captured. And they were bitter because the Chinese had failed to support them with spare parts, maintenance equipment, or trained ground crews.

In these aerial encounters Boyington chalked up a score of six enemy fighters downed, several of them Zeros. The Zeros were better planes than the P-40s, but Boyington happened to be a better combat pilot than his foes. In a fight between near-equal aircraft, it was the man in the cockpit who made the difference.

But by the spring of 1942 Boyington had become fed up with the Chinese government's broken promises that the Flying Tigers would get more planes, more parts and equipment, better ground crews. He decided he would use the clause in his marine resignation papers that allowed him to rejoin the corps if the United States went to war. He hitchhiked by air to Bombay, India, and caught a passenger ship to New York.

Pappy Boyington, Marine Corps major, climbs into Black Sheep squadron plane on way to dogfight with Japanese Zero fighters.

He applied for reinstatement at once, but it was a long time coming. Without money in his pocket, he had to work as a car parker in a Manhattan garage for seventy-five cents an hour while he waited for months. Finally, in desperation he fired off a three-page night letter to the assistant secretary of the navy.

In three days Boyington had his orders and the rank of major, and was off to San Diego, California. From there he was shipped to the South Pacific. At twenty-nine Boyington was a few years older than his flying companions. In deference to his years they nicknamed him "Pappy."

Boyington's first stop was at Espíritu Santo, an island in the New Hebrides group. There he served as operations officer for an outfit supplying the fighter squadrons on Guadalcanal. Then he did a short tour of duty as squadron leader on Guadalcanal itself. Unfortunately he broke his ankle in a barroom fracas and had to spend long weeks in a New Zealand hospital.

Back at his old job on Espíritu Santo, Boyington kept pleading for a more active role. His request was soon granted. He was named squadron leader in a larger group that headed for the Russell Islands. Boyington was flying one of twenty Corsairs that escorted three squadrons of Dauntless dive bombers and two squadrons of Avenger torpedo planes. Their mission: to wipe out the Japanese installation on Ballale, one that controlled all air traffic in the area.

Over Ballale the marine pilots tangled with a host of Zeros while protecting their own bombers. It was like a World War I dogfight—every man for himself, Corsairs and Zeros each maneuvering for the best angle of attack. Boyington shot down five Zeros before he retreated, his fuel and ammunition almost gone.

Back at the base Boyington's squadron, bloodied in their first combat flight together, searched for a squadron name. They finally came up with "Black Sheep" and had name and insignia painted on all their aircraft. The Black Sheep continued to fly as escorts, especially on the mission to retake Bougainville, northernmost of the Solomon Islands.

Often the marines encountered Japanese fighter defenses as well as strong antiaircraft fire. They suffered many losses, but shot down even more enemy planes. By December 1943 Boyington's kill record had risen to twenty-five, only one less than the tally racked up by Rickenbacker in World War I.

On January 3, 1944, in a raid over Rabaul, two things happened to Boyington. He broke Rickenbacker's record and he was shot down. After scoring against two Zeros, he came down in the water. The Japanese kept shooting at him as he fumbled with his life raft. He stayed afloat on the raft for eight hours, tending to his wounds and paddling for shore. Before he could reach land, he was picked up by a Japanese submarine and taken prisoner.

Ashore in Rabaul, Boyington underwent an intensive grilling. He revealed only his name and rank. He didn't have a serial number; none had been given him when he reentered the marine corps. He was held for six weeks in a filthy cell in Rabaul, his wounds untreated. Then, with five other American prisoners of war, he was flown to Japan.

Boyington was held in Camp Ofuna, near Yokohama. His jailers ordered him to keep himself and his cell neat and clean—and they beat him unmercifully with a baseball bat when he refused to answer questions. His weight fell from 180 to 110 pounds.

He even went without drinking for a year. His forced

abstinence was broken only once, when he was working in the camp kitchen. He induced the guards to give him some of their New Year's party *sake*, a potent Japanese wine.

In February 1945 the United States began a heavy air bombardment of Japan. Boyington cheered the American planes he saw overhead, even though the bombs dropped uncomfortably close to Camp Ofuna. In April he and seventeen other American captives were shifted to Camp Omouri, where they sweated out the rest of the war.

Thin, still limping from an injury sustained when he leaped from his plane at Rabaul, Boyington won his freedom when Japan surrendered. He also claimed a Congressional Medal of Honor awarded him three months after his plane had been found floating in the sea off Rabaul.

At that time Boyington had been listed as "missing, presumed dead." Now he was safe and very much alive.

CHAPTER 13
DAUNTLESS WOMEN OF THE AIR

AMELIA EARHART, JACQUELINE COCHRAN, HANNA REITSCH

When Wilbur Wright was in France in 1908, trying to sell manufacturing rights to the Wright *Flyer*, he hired a sales representative named Hart Berg. Berg had already shown his ability by selling American submarine and automobile manufacturing rights to the French.

One of Berg's goals was to generate public enthusiasm for the *Flyer*. So he set up a demonstration site near the racetrack at Le Mans. Now—how to get the racetrack crowds interested in watching the demonstration? Berg dreamed up a unique stunt. He brought his wife, Edith, to Le Mans and seated her in the *Flyer*, right up there with Wilbur Wright.

And there she perched, skirts tied around her knees, when Wright took the *Flyer* 50 feet into the air. He kept the plane aloft for more than two minutes, his passenger holding on tightly but smiling delightedly the whole time.

Wilbur Wright got his signed contracts from the French. And Edith Berg became the first woman to have gone up in an airplane. She opened the door for women in aviation, a door that keeps opening wider and wider.

Today there are no real barriers that prevent women from piloting aircraft. They fly tiny Piper Cubs and giant 747s. They fly all types of military aircraft. Except in actual combat tests, they have proved that they can fly any kind of airplane.

Achieving equal flight status with men was the result of a long battle, part of the general struggle for equal rights for all women. Starting with Edith Berg, a host of able women fliers have amply demonstrated that sex discrimination has no place in aviation. Each year an increasing number of women are graduated from the U.S. Air Force Academy qualified to fly the most complex military aircraft.

The first woman to be granted a pilot's license was Harriet Quimby, age twenty-seven. In 1911 she took her biplane to the headquarters of the Aero Club, in those days the licensing agency. The Aero Club didn't know what to do. It had never licensed a woman before.

Harriet Quimby gently insisted on her right to apply. And to demonstrate her flying ability she took her plane up, circled the field, and put it down only eight feet from the takeoff point. She got her license. "Flying seems easier than voting," she told a group of reporters. (Women didn't get the right to vote in national elections until 1920.)

Only a year later Quimby was killed in a flight accident. She was over Dorchester Bay in Boston, coming back from a speed trial around Boston Lighthouse. Suddenly her plane stalled, then plunged toward the water.

Some force ejected Quimby from the falling plane.

She went down swiftly into the bay, the plane following closely after her, and she was drowned. When the plane was recovered, the aneroid barometer showed an altitude of more than 5,000 feet. This was higher than any other woman had ever flown.

Amelia Earhart, Famous for Firsts

WOMEN CONTINUED to earn their wings quietly, without making waves. They set speed, distance, and altitude records that nearly matched men's marks. But none commanded real headlines until Amelia Earhart came along.

AE, as her husband and friends called her, established a number of famous firsts in aviation. A notable one was "first woman to fly solo across the Atlantic." Her name is always included in any list of renowned fliers.

Born in Kansas, AE moved often as a child with her family. Her father was a railroad claims agent who kept getting fired because of his drinking habits. Thus every few years he had to locate a new job in another town. After she grew to young womanhood, AE kept shifting from job to job herself, trying to find her own identity. In time she did find herself in aviation, a career that exactly suited her restless, adventure-seeking nature.

She learned to fly in Los Angeles a few years after the end of World War I. She was working in a Boston settlement house, flying on weekends, when she was asked if she'd like to go along as a member of a flight team that was set to cross the Atlantic. This was in 1928, only a year after Lindbergh made his famous flight. Earhart accepted the invitation at once.

The plane, a tri-motor Fokker, had a capable pilot

and flight mechanic. AE had little to do but keep the flight log. Nevertheless, by the time they reached Britain she was already famous, wildly acclaimed as the first woman to cross the Atlantic by air. She enjoyed her popularity, wrote a book about the flight, and endorsed several products, earning a good deal of money. And she married George Palmer Putnam, one of the flight promoters.

AE had really been only a passenger on this Atlantic crossing. She felt the increasing need to establish herself as a pilot in her own right. So in 1932 she set up a solo Atlantic flight, with herself in the pilot's seat. Flying from Harbor Grace, Newfoundland, to Londonderry, Northern Ireland, she made the trip in fifteen hours, eighteen minutes, more than five hours faster than the 1928 flight.

Again she was met by cheers, parades, banquets, the whole galaxy of public praise. This time, however, the honors were for her own skill and daring, not merely for going along for the ride. During the next and last five years of her short life, her fame never flagged.

Amelia Earhart stands before plane in hangar at March Field, California. She was lost, presumably drowned, on flight around the world.

In these ensuing years she made a number of pioneer flights. She spent a year as "aviatrix-in-residence" at Purdue University. At the end of the spring term the Purdue Research Foundation presented her with a Lockheed 10-E Electra. She soon decided what she would do with the plane: in it she would fly around the world.

After a false start, Earhart and her navigator, Fred Noonan, got going on May 20, 1937. Stopping often for the night at points along the way, they crossed the United States and flew south to Natal, Brazil. From there they crossed the Atlantic, putting down at Dakar in what was then French West Africa.

By stages AE and Noonan traversed the African continent, then flew across India, and down to the north coast of Australia. From there they prepared to cross the broad Pacific. Stopping in New Guinea to top off their fuel supply, they set out for Howland Island in the central Pacific.

Howland Island, only two miles long and a half-mile wide, was a mere pinpoint in the vast ocean. They never found it. Somewhere close to Howland, their radio failed, and they apparently ran out of fuel. They probably ditched their plane in the sea and were drowned.

But there are those who say that AE was on a secret intelligence assignment—to learn how the Japanese-held islands in the central Pacific were being prepared for the war that was coming soon. The story goes that Earhart and Noonan were actually flying over the Japanese islands when they were forced down and taken prisoner. Perhaps, sooner or later, they were executed.

The White House, the State Department, and the Department of Defense have never commented on these speculations. The official silence suggests there might be some truth in the stories.

Jacqueline Cochran and her WASPs

AMERICAN WOMEN pilots served their country effectively and well in World War II. As WASPs—Women's Airforce Service Pilots—they ferried all kinds of military aircraft all across the nation. Doing so, they relieved male pilots for combat duty. The WASP chief was Jacqueline Cochran, skilled as both pilot and businesswoman.

Jacqueline Cochran never knew exactly how old she was. Nor did she ever learn who her real parents were. She was the foster child of a family who lived in the sawmill towns of northern Florida. When she was about eight her family moved to Columbus, Georgia, where the small girl worked twelve hours a night in a cotton mill. She attended school for only two years and learned to read and write on her own.

In her early teens Cochran switched from the cotton mill to a local beauty shop. Soon she was cutting and styling hair. She was giving permanent waves when one of her customers talked her into studying nursing. After training, she worked for a doctor.

Cochran's heart was not in nursing as a career. She went back to the beauty business, working for a concern with fashionable shops in New York and Miami. In 1932 she met Floyd Odlum, a millionaire financier. To Odlum she confessed her dream of owning her own cosmetics company. Odlum told her that to run such a business successfully, she would have to learn to fly.

In the summer of 1932 Cochran took flying lessons and got her license. She flew in many air races, often finishing first. And in 1936 she married Floyd Odlum. After AE disappeared, Cochran became America's No. 1 woman pilot.

World War II was on its way. As soon as Poland fell in 1939 Cochran wrote to Eleanor Roosevelt, the President's wife, telling her of the role that women pilots could play in releasing men for combat flying. The time to begin thinking about all this, Cochran suggested, was now. As war grew nearer for the United States, she kept pushing for a women's air auxiliary.

In March 1941 Cochran learned that pilots were needed to fly American-built Lockheed Hudson bombers to Britain. Britain could furnish no fliers for the task. General H. H. Arnold, U.S. Army Air Corps chief, suggested to Cochran that she ask for the job. She did. Months passed and nothing happened. Then she applied pressure to one of Britain's top war officials. In June she was invited to Montreal for flight tests.

Cochran was given the green light as pilot, but only under the condition that her copilot, a man, would handle the controls during takeoff and landing. She had to accept the compromise. The flight was a success, and in Britain Cochran conferred with Pauline Gower, chief of the women pilots in Britain's Air Transport Auxiliary.

On her return Cochran was invited to lunch with Pres-

Jacqueline Cochran, after winning Bendix Prize race. During World War II she headed the women's flight service.

ident and Mrs. Roosevelt. She left the luncheon party with a note from the President to Robert Lovett, the assistant secretary of war for air. The note said that Jacqueline Cochran was to begin planning a women pilots' organization that would work with the U.S. Army Air Corps. The first hurdle had been overcome.

At the beginning only a few women pilots had the licenses and the certified hours of flight that the army air corps said were needed to be a military flier. By December 1941, when the United States entered the fighting, there were fewer than two hundred women fliers who could qualify. So the big task was to train women for the many flight duties demanded of them.

For two and a half years Jacqueline Cochran processed more than 25,000 applications from women who had already taken lessons at civilian flying schools. From these she selected a total of 1,830 candidates who then took six months of training at Avenger Field in Sweetwater, Texas, the nation's only all-female air base. Of these 1,830 candidates, 1,074 completed the course.

The Avenger Field graduates flew a total of sixty million miles during World War II. They piloted everything from the P-51 fighter to the B-29 Superfort. From manufacturing plants they ferried thousands of planes to American seaports for shipment to fighting fronts. They towed target sleeves for gunnery practice. They tested all sorts of craft, from training planes to the first experimental jets. And they passed every kind of physical exam devised by the surgeon general to test the reactions of women flying under stress.

Of course Cochran encountered much opposition from high military brass and from prominent congressmen.

Some simply couldn't believe that women could perform men's jobs with any efficiency. Others were jealous that they could. Cochran did her best to silence such criticism, but much of it persisted. Her best argument was to let the WASP record speak for itself. She knew that controversy, however pointless, could help destroy the WASP organization.

For example, in 1943 a WASP-piloted plane went down in North Carolina, killing the pilot in the crash. Investigation turned up traces of sugar in the gas tank that seriously hurt engine performance. Cochran could have pressed for further investigation.

She didn't. She realized that a widely publicized scandal would hurt the WASP organization even more than it would hurt the group's enemies. Thirty-eight women lost their lives flying for the WASP. But none of these deaths provided a reason for criticizing the WASP organization itself.

Despite Cochran's intense lobbying, Congress never made the WASP an official part of America's armed forces during World War II. They were treated as civilian workers under contract. It was not until 1977 that Congress passed a law declaring the WASP to be veterans, entitled to all veterans' benefits. Cochran's long fight for full acceptance had been won.

In the years after World War II Cochran kept on flying. She set more than two hundred flight records in her career. In 1953 she was the first woman pilot to break the sound barrier, flying an F-86 jet fighter. In 1961 she established a new women's altitude record of 55,253 feet, and in the following year a new woman's speed record of 1,429 miles an hour. She died in 1980.

Hanna Reitsch, Ace German Aviatrix

GERMANY, LIKE the Allied nations, had no women fliers in its regular ranks during World War II. One woman, however, scored spectacular feats as a pilot. She was a close friend of Adolf Hitler as well. Her name was Hanna Reitsch.

Reitsch was the first pilot, man or woman, to fly a glider over the Alps. She was the first woman helicopter pilot in Germany and the first German woman test pilot. She established more than 40 endurance and altitude records and in 1942 she was the first woman to win the highly prized Iron Cross.

Hanna Reitsch was the pilot of the last plane that flew out of Berlin just before the city fell to the Soviet onslaught in 1945. Behind that last flight lies a dramatic story.

In the final days before Germany fell, Fuhrer Adolf Hitler was holed up in a bunker buried in the rubble of the savaged Chancellory building in Berlin. He was nearly crazy, out of touch with reality, still deluding himself that the Nazis would win the war. He ordered Colonel-General Ritter von Greim, a top air force official stationed in Munich, to report to him in the bunker.

It was Hanna Reitsch who flew Greim to Berlin. For most of the way she had to fly at treetop level to avoid being spotted in the sky. Hitler met them at the door of the bunker. Reitsch recalled how the Fuhrer looked:

"His head sagged, his face was deadly pallid, and the uncontrollable shaking of his hands made the message from Göring [the number two Nazi] flutter wildly as he handed it to Greim."

That same night Hitler gave Reitsch a vial of poison,

saying: "Hanna, you belong to those who will die with me. Each of us has a vial of poison such as this. I do not wish that one of us falls into the hands of the Russians alive, nor do I wish our bodies to be found by them."

In a few minutes Hitler's mood changed. He reassured Reitsch that German armies were rushing in from the south and all would be well.

She stayed in the bunker for four days. Then Hitler commanded Greim and Reitsch to fly out of Berlin. They were to carry orders for the arrest of Heinrich Himmler, another high Nazi. "A traitor must never succecd me as Fuhrer," Hitler shouted. "You must go out to insure that he will not."

This time Reitsch flew at an altitude of 20,000 feet to escape Allied antiaircraft fire. They failed to find Himmler, but they did stop in several German cities to deliver messages from the bunker inhabitants. The onrushing Allied forces soon put a stop to that. Reitsch surrendered to the Americans. She was held for about a year, partly because of the rumor that she had flown Hitler to South America, a rumor that was not substantiated. Then she was released.

Reitsch continued to fly after the war. In 1962 she set up a glider school in Ghana, the African nation led by Kwame Nkrumah. The school folded in 1966 when Nkrumah was overthrown. Reitsch died in 1979 at the age of 67.

CHAPTER

DESTROYING HITLER'S INDUSTRIAL MIGHT

GUY GIBSON

The Allied landings at Normandy on the north coast of France were the beginning of the end of World War II in Europe. First the big guns of Allied warships pulverized the coast. Then Allied planes strafed and rocketed it, raking it over almost inch by inch. Still, the Allied ground forces had to storm their way ashore and struggle to gain a foothold. It was a mammoth undertaking, at a huge cost in men, munitions, and equipment. And it was successful.

The landings began on June 6, 1944, nearly five years after World War II started. For much of those five years Allied planes were engaged in attempting to weaken the hold of the Nazis on the European continent. With their fighter escorts, bomber formations roared over industrial cities in Germany and its captive countries. The targets of these bombers were arms plants, airfields, railroad junctions, seaports—any place that aided the Nazi war effort.

Guy Gibson and His Dam Busters

ONE OF these targets presented extremely difficult problems to the British air strategists. The man chosen to help solve those problems was Squadron Commander Guy Penrose Gibson, age twenty-four.

Young Gibson was born in India. His father, a British civil servant, was conservator of forests there. Gibson was reared in England and attended St. Edward's School, Oxford. (Douglas Bader was an earlier St. Edward's graduate.) Chunky, broad, muscular, Gibson stopped growing when he was only a few inches above five feet.

Gibson's early ambition was to become a test pilot. After graduation from St. Edward's, he applied to an aircraft plant for such a post. He was advised to join the RAF to get needed experience. At first the RAF told him he was too short. He went home to stretch and exercise. Reapplying, he was accepted—barely.

Gibson became a crackerjack flier. He was ready and waiting when war came in 1939. A bomber pilot, he fought hard and well in the Battle of Britain. Later, he took time out to marry an actress named Evelyn Moore. Their brief times together were ecstatically happy, and they looked forward to the end of the war when they could be together.

In fact, it was at the end of his 173rd mission, a bombing raid over Stuttgart, Germany, that Gibson thought he'd be granted leave. He wanted to go to the south of England, where he and Evelyn had a country house. There he could relax and put the war out of mind for several days at least. But it was already 1943, and British night bombing raids over continental Europe were taking place constantly.

So, instead of granting him leave immediately after the Stuttgart flight, Gibson's chief asked him if he'd like "to do one more trip." Gibson saw his leave go flying out the window, but he couldn't say no to the request.

The chief could tell Gibson nothing about the mission or the target except that it was so important that a special squadron was to be formed, and Gibson was to organize that squadron.

Gibson went right to work. He picked 147 men (later cut to 133) and set them up into twenty-one crews (later cut to nineteen) of what was to become the No. 617 Squadron. At the squadron's first meeting Gibson told the men only that they were soon to take off on a secret raid over Germany and that they were to practice flying low "until you know how to do it with your eyes shut."

In fact, that was about all Gibson himself knew of the mission at the moment. He was soon to learn more. The man who eventually told him about the intended targets was a scientist named Dr. Barnes N. Wallis.

Dr. Wallis was a student of bombing. Right from the start of the war he planned to drop superbombs on Germany's heavily industrial areas. One of these was the Ruhr Valley. It contained factories, steel refineries, mills, and at least three important dams: the Mohne, the Sorpe, and the Eder.

The first two dams supplied about three quarters of the Ruhr's household and industrial needs. The Mohne, by itself, dammed up a lake twelve miles long. If the dam were cracked by bombing, it would flood the valley with 140 million tons of water. The Eder was a hydroelectric power source. It held back about 200 million tons of water.

But no ordinary bomb dropped in an ordinary way

could destroy these dams. First, the bomb had to be at least five tons in weight, shaped like a cylinder, and made of special high explosives. Second, it had to spin, or revolve, when dropped into the lake abutting the dam. On hitting the water surface, it had to shoot forward until it struck the dam. Then, still spinning, it had to drop to the right depth along the face of the dam. There it was to explode. The explosion, aided by the pressure of the water at that depth, would be tremendous enough to blow up the dam.

Dr. Wallis had experimented and made dummy trials of his bomb. With these he got the reluctant consent of the RAF brass to go ahead. It was at this time, in February 1943, that Gibson was assigned to organize and train No. 617 Squadron. Dr. Wallis told Gibson that his pilots would have to approach the target at a speed of 240 miles an hour and an altitude of 2,000 feet, then dive to within 150 feet of the water and drop the bomb.

Only later did Dr. Wallis tell Gibson that the targets were to be three dams in the Ruhr Valley. Dr. Wallis described the solidity and strength of the dams: 140 feet thick, 150 feet high, made of solid concrete and masonry. He told Gibson that the strikes must be made when the water was within four feet of the tops of the dams. The water would reach that level in about six weeks. Could Gibson be ready by then?

Gibson could, and training was intensified. The pilots were taught simple methods to calculate when and where to release the bombs. Almost at the last minute Dr. Wallis changed his mind about the height from which the bombs should be dropped. Now he wanted them released from an altitude of only fifty feet instead of the 150 feet he had specified earlier. This meant flying very low over the dams. Gibson, his heart in his mouth, said he would follow orders.

By May 13, 1943, all nineteen Lancasters had been delivered to the base and their 133 crewmen thoroughly briefed. A bomb was taken aboard each Lancaster and placed next to the motor that was to start it spinning as it dropped.

The squadron took off on the night of May 16. It was divided into three waves. The first, made up of nine Lancasters, was to aim for the Mohne dam. The second, consisting of five planes, was to go after the Sorpe. The third wave of another five planes was to be held in reserve.

The first wave followed a track across southern Holland. One Lancaster was shot down as the wave flew too near a fortified German airfield. The other eight planes crossed the Rhine River and were soon above the Ruhr Valley.

Gibson, in the lead Lancaster, began positioning his aircraft for the bombing run over the Mohne dam. His navigator checked their height above the lake. His bombardier got the dam within his sights. The motor designed to spin the bomb was turned on. Meantime, German gun defenses on the dam began blazing away at the oncoming aircraft.

The bomb was dropped. It hit precisely where it was aimed and sent water shooting a thousand feet high. But nothing else happened—the dam itself remained intact. Gibson ordered the next plane in line to make its run.

Before it could reach the target, this next plane was hit by antiaircraft fire. It dropped its bomb too late, then crashed into the ground beyond the dam. The bombardier and the rear gunner survived. The other five crewmen were killed in the crash.

DESTROYING HITLER'S INDUSTRIAL MIGHT /163

Bombs from planes three and four also failed to destroy the dam. But the bomb from plane five struck home. Suddenly the dam gave way, and an ocean of water gushed into the Ruhr Valley. It swept away everything in its path —houses, factories, every seemingly solid, rooted thing. Gibson's radioman at once reported the news to Dr. Wallis and others at the squadron base in England. They received the news with wild delight.

Of the original nine Lancasters, seven were still in the air, but only three still had their bombs. Gibson ordered two of the bomb-expended planes back to base. The other two, his own, and the deputy leader's plane remained. Followed by the three bomb-armed planes, they led the attack on the Eder dam.

The Eder proved to be a harder target to hit than the Mohne. Right in the bomb run hovered a medieval castle. The bombing plane would have to clear the castle, dive suddenly from a 1,000-foot altitude to 50 feet, drop the bomb, then climb quickly to avoid crashing into a mountain looming just beyond.

The first plane made at least five tries, but broke away before dropping its bomb. The second plane made two unsuccessful attempts. On its third run it dropped the bomb too late. It struck the top of the dam, then exploded.

The third plane made one run, then a second. The second one worked. The Eder dam was breached, sending millions of tons of water shooting through the valley. The deluge swamped everything in its path. To Gibson the devastation looked even greater than that caused by the Mohne break.

Meantime, the second wave of five Lancasters had taken off to bomb the Sorpe. It met with failure. Two of the planes were shot down, two were hit by flak and had to limp back to the base, and only the fifth actually dropped its bomb. It damaged the Sorpe, but the dam did not burst.

The five planes in the third wave—the one in reserve—were activated when Gibson radioed that all his bombs had been dropped. One plane was sent to attack the Lister dam, but was shot down before it reached the target. Three planes were dispatched to the Sorpe to cash in on the damage caused by the second wave plane.

Of these, one Lancaster was shot down over Holland. Another dropped its bomb but failed to shake the Sorpe. The third found the target area shrouded by fog and could not make the run. The fifth reserve Lancaster was sent to the Schwelm dam. It dropped its bomb in the right place, but no damage resulted.

Nineteen Lancasters of the No. 617 Squadron went out that fateful night of May 16–17, 1943. Eight never came back. Fifty-six men served as crews of these lost aircraft. Only two returned alive. As historians put it, the attack was "a costly success."

The dam's destruction caused immense havoc. About a thousand people were drowned, and two hundred more remained missing. Horses, cows, sheep, and pigs were swept away by the floods, and thousands of acres of cropland were inundated. Industry and transportation were crippled. Water for drinking and for industrial use was in short supply.

But the Germans were very resourceful. They replaced the lost workers with "slave" laborers from captive countries. They cleared away the rubble and built new factories. The Ruhr Valley remained Germany's chief industrial supplier until the nation surrendered in May 1945.

After the dam raid Guy Gibson celebrated its success with his remaining comrades-at-arms. Then, with a heavy heart, he sat down to write brief notes of condolence to the relatives of the fifty-four who had perished in the raid. For his part, Gibson was awarded the Victoria Cross to add to his previously earned Distinguished Service Order and Distinguished Flying Cross.

Gibson spent a long leave with Evelyn, his wife. Then he went with Prime Minister Winston Churchill on a tour of the United States, strengthening British ties to America. Many friends thought he had contributed enough as a flier. They urged him to retire to a good job in private business or even to run for Parliament.

But peace was still a long way off, and Gibson chose to remain in the RAF. He returned to active duty as base operations officer of No. 627 Squadron. On September 19–20, 1944, he commanded a raid on an industrial plant in the Ruhr. Flying a Mosquito, he directed his Lancasters as they bombed the target. Mission completed, he told his planes to return home.

Gibson himself never made it back. His Mosquito crashed into a hillside, and he died instantly.

CHAPTER **15**
PILOTS OF THE DIVINE WIND

For much of its early history, Japan remained apart from the rest of the world, even from its close neighbor, China. Isolated by choice, the Japanese people developed a life-style all their own. It was as if they were the sole occupants of another planet, away from the earth. Even after Japan opened its doors to trade with other countries in the 1860s, the people's way of life continued unchanged.

In fact, that life-style lasted until the end of World War II. Only then did the Japanese people realize that many of their beliefs and attitudes were mistaken, and that these very beliefs and attitudes had helped lead to their defeat in war.

One of their beliefs was that the Japanese emperor was divine. Most of the people felt that he had been appointed to rule Japan by the heavenly powers. His war directives were considered holy and had to be obeyed.

The war directives were really written by Japan's ruling generals and admirals. In one sense, these military leaders considered the emperor a puppet, not a god. They used him as a "front man" in their schemes to rule the whole Pacific and the Far East.

Yet in another sense, the generals and admirals were completely loyal to their emperor. Despite the way they manipulated him, they thought of him as a symbol from heaven needed to bless Japan as it sought to take over much of the world. That's why many of them committed *hara-kiri* (suicide) when they failed to accomplish a mission. It was better to die, they believed, than to face the emperor with an admission of defeat.

For the same reason, a Japanese soldier taken prisoner was filled with shame and self-loathing. He much preferred to die in battle "for the emperor" rather than to surrender. He, too, often committed hara-kiri, believing he would reach the special heaven reserved for soldiers loyal to the throne.

The majority of Japanese also believed that things of the spirit were stronger than things of the flesh. Although America's guns and planes were better than Japan's, the Japanese spirit was superior to that of the American and would eventually triumph.

This was one reason why Japan refused to accept defeat until the very end, in August 1945. Yet by the fall of 1944 Japan was definitely losing the war in the Pacific. At the war's beginning Japan had conquered and commanded the chain of Pacific islands that stretched from just north of Australia to Japan itself. It also held Indochina, Indonesia, and much of east China.

But American forces moving northward had retaken most of these islands. Now in the autumn of 1944 they were in control of the Marianas (Guam, Saipan, Tinian) and had landed on Leyte in the Philippines. The retreating Japanese army was on the run.

From air bases in the Marianas and the Philippines, the Americans were ready to send giant B-29s to bomb industrial cities on the Japanese home islands. Japanese civilians had not seen U.S. bombers overhead since Doolittle's Raiders had stung them two and a half years earlier. They were soon to face a rain of destruction from the sky.

At sea, American carrier-based aircraft had sunk or badly crippled dozens of Japanese warships. The Japanese fleet was gutted, incapable of striking back in any force. The once proud air force was in shambles. It had few planes or experienced pilots left.

Japanese military experts figured that their chief enemy was the American aircraft carrier. From its flight deck, fighters and bombers took off to sink or scuttle every Japanese ship, plane, or ground force in sight. How could these carriers be stopped?

Ohnishi's Answer

THE ANSWER—a wildy desperate and eventually useless one—came from Vice-Admiral Takajiro Ohnishi, new commander of the First Air Fleet, based near Manila in the Philippines, in October 1944. Ohnishi was a strong leader of the younger officers under him. His equals and superiors thought him conceited and stubborn, but his juniors almost worshiped him.

Ohnishi studied the men and material he had just taken over. He saw shabby and poorly maintained planes, and pilots equally shabby and poor in spirit. His solution came like a bombshell.

Ohnishi's plan was to organize a group of fliers who would crash their bomb-laden Zeros into the flight decks of U.S. carriers. A direct hit would seriously damage the carrier, perhaps even sink it. The least it could do would be to put the carrier in the repair docks for weeks.

Of course, the pilot would die in the crash.

Both pilot and plane were to be called *kamikaze* (kah-mih-KAH-zee). The word meant "divine wind" and came from a thirteenth century story in which the Mongol emperor, Kublai Khan, attempted to invade Japan from the sea. A "divine wind" (probably a typhoon) arose, sinking some of the khan's ships and scattering the rest. Japan was miraculously saved by the kamikaze. Now the Kamikaze Special Attack Force would save Japan again.

Or so many thought. Among young fliers the proposal caught on like wildfire. Now they had something to die for, a purpose for their self-sacrifice. Ohnishi's aides quickly organized a kamikaze unit and gave him an announcement to sign. Posted on October 20, 1944, it read:

The 201st Air Group will organize a special attack corps and will destroy or disable, if possible by 25 October, the enemy carrier forces in the waters east of the Philippines.
The corps will be called the *Shimpu Attack Unit*. It will consist of 26 fighter planes, of which half will be assigned to crash-diving missions, and the remainder to escort, and will be divided into four sections, designated as follows: Shikishima, Yamato, Asahi, and Yamazakura.
The Shimpu Attack Unit will be commanded by Lieutenant Yukio Seki.

(*Shimpu* is another way of saying "kamikaze." *Shikishima* is a poetic name for Japan. *Yamato* is the ancient name of Japan. *Ahasi* means "morning sun." *Yamazakura* means "mountain cherry blossoms." The Japanese have always expressed themselves poetically.)

The Yamato squadron prepared itself for an attack at Cebu, an island some distance from Leyte. The other squadrons were to perform their missions on the carriers at Leyte Gulf.

On their foreheads, beneath their helmets, the kamikaze pilots wore the white cloth that linked them with the *samurai*, Japan's ancient warrior caste.

Before they took off, Admiral Ohnishi told them: "You are already gods, without earthly desires. But one thing you want to know is that your crash dive is not in vain. Regrettably, we will not be able to tell you the results. But I shall watch your efforts to the end and report your deeds to the Throne. You may all rest assured on this point. I ask you all to do your best."

To "report your deeds" to the emperor—this was all the kamikaze pilots had to know. Now they were more willing than ever to sacrifice their lives. Before taking off, Lieutenant Seki, the unit commander, gave one of the senior officers an envelope containing a lock of his hair. This was to be sent to his wife and mother as a memorial token.

Death took a holiday that morning. The kamikazes could find no targets. Nor could they for the next three mornings. Finally, on October 25, they hit the small carrier *Saint Lo* and sank it.

The returning escort planes reported a great victory. American losses were greatly exaggerated, but from these the Japanese admirals concluded that the kamikaze was the only weapon that would turn defeat into victory.

PILOTS OF THE DIVINE WIND /171

Ohnishi demanded three hundred more planes and as many pilots. He needed these, he claimed, to complete the task. He was given about half the number he wanted. The planes he got were in poor repair, the pilots young and only half-trained.

The new kamikaze pilots were sent to the island of Formosa (now called Taiwan) for a week's training on how to commit their last attack with maximum effect. They soon went into action.

Diving into carriers around the Philippines, the kamikazes scored some spectacular hits. They sank several ships and badly damaged others. But they could not stop the Americans from completing their conquest of the Philippines.

Next American stop: the island of Iwo Jima, less than 800 miles from Japan. The Americans were victorious, but only after weeks of pre-invasion offshore bombardment by U.S. warships, followed by a marine invasion of the island. During the weeks of hand-to-hand struggle, about 5,000 Americans were killed. So were more than 20,000 Japanese. As the land fighting went on, American ships in Iwo Jima's waters were peppered by kamikaze attacks.

Okinawa is one of the Ryuku Islands, lying about 350 miles south of Japan. In March 1945 the big guns of American warships laid siege to Okinawa, softening it up for the invasion that began April 1. As the marines and army men fought their way ashore and across the island, the ships continued to fire over their heads until Okinawa was completely under American control. The U.S. forces lost more than 12,000, but the Japanese suffered a staggering toll of more than 100,000 dead.

At Okinawa the kamikazes were out in full force. They were making a last-ditch effort to keep from going down to defeat and to what they were convinced would be miserable degradation. Here the Japanese revealed a new kamikaze weapon. This was the Ohka ("cherry blossom") bomb.

Actually, the Ohka was a glider twenty feet long with wings sixteen feet wide. It had rocket boosters in its tail and a ton of high explosives in its nose. A bomber carried the Ohka under its fuselage to a point near the target. Then the kamikaze pilot climbed down from the bomber into the tiny cockpit of the Ohka. Released from the bomber, the Ohka—using its rockets—reached a speed of 500 miles an hour as it struck an American ship.

The Ohka never became a fearsome weapon. About eight hundred were manufactured, but only fifty were used in kamikaze attacks. And only three ever hit U.S. vessels. No wonder American sailors changed the name Ohka ("cherry blossom") to Baka ("stupid").

Surrounding Okinawa as the invasion proceeded were about 1,500 American ships, large and small, as well as 22 British vessels. The Japanese were determined to sink most of them. This, they figured, would stop the reinforcement of the invading troops and soon defeat them.

So they organized a *Kikusui* ("floating chrysanthemum") attack by kamikazes. It began on April 6, 1945, when hundreds of Kikusui pilots and planes flung themselves at the American ships around Okinawa. Other hundreds of Hellcats, Helldivers, Avengers, and other carrier-based planes rose to meet them. Aided by antiaircraft fire from the U.S. vessels, the Hellcats and others succeeded in knocking the kamikazes out of the sky before they could do much damage. But about twenty slipped through and caused immense harm.

Despite great losses, the Kikusui attacks, ten in all,

continued almost to the day the island was won. Their major targets were the U.S. destroyers acting as radar picket ships. The pickets patrolled the outskirts of the assembled U.S. fleet and used their radar to detect oncoming ships and planes. The kamikazes succeeded in sinking many of those destroyers.

After the third Kikusui attack, Radio Tokyo told the Japanese people that 217 American warships had been sunk. The true figure was only 14. During the whole Okinawa campaign, only 17 American ships were destroyed. It cost Japan the lives of 930 kamikaze to sink those ships.

These American losses, although serious, had little effect on the accumulation of U.S. air and sea power that was relentlessly closing in on Japan. Stronger than ever, the U.S. forces now stood at Okinawa ready for the final assault on Japan itself. The desperate kamikaze attacks had been useless.

Even now, long decades after World War II, it is difficult to understand what went on in the minds of the kamikaze pilots. In the record of history's wars are many true stories of fighting men who sacrificed their own lives to save their comrades or to win a crucial battle. But these willing decisions to die were made mainly during crises, under immense emotional pressure.

The kamikaze decisions, by contrast, were made calmly, many days or weeks before the suicide attacks were to take place. The pilots were trained in the most effective ways to die—how to trade their lives for the biggest possible gains. They had a long time to consider what they were going to do. Few, if any, backed down.

The pilots' families knew all about the intended fate of their sons, brothers, husbands. There is no evidence that they tried to interfere. The families agreed that to die for the emperor under such conditions was the noblest act a young man could perform. It would surely lead him into heaven.

The last entry in the diary of a kamikaze pilot who soon flew to his death tells us his point of view:

> Like cherry blossoms
> In the spring
> Let us fall
> Clean and radiant.

CHAPTER **16**
DESTRUCTION FROM THE SKIES

Starting in March 1945, even before American troops landed on Okinawa beaches, the B-29 Superforts were bombing Tokyo into rubble and ruins. The B-29 was the biggest combat plane the army air force had ever sent aloft.

It was 99 feet long, nearly 28 feet high, and had a wing-span of more than 141 feet. Painted silver, it had four engines. It could cover a distance of 3,500 miles carrying five tons of bombs. Its cruising speed was 350 miles an hour. The B-29 was an awesome weapon.

But the B-29 was also new and untried. During the first few months of its operations in the Pacific, the B-29s suffered too many crashes, too many aborted flights. General Curtis LeMay, chief of the Twenty-first Bomber Command that flew the B-29s, determined to find out why. He decided that the planes were carrying too many guns and that they were flying too high.

LeMay wanted to check out his decision. So he organized a huge flight of 325 B-29s, all their guns removed. Their destination: Tokyo. Their task: to fly low, not over 5,000 feet, and drop thousands of tons of incendiary bombs on a concentrated factory district.

From its Guam base the flight took off in the early evening of March 9. It reached Tokyo about midnight. At altitudes of just a few thousand feet, the bombardiers released their fire bombs with blazing accuracy.

Whole streets of homes and factories shot up in flames, totally destroyed within minutes. High winds aided in the wipeout. People ran from their burning houses only to be consumed by the fires that swept through the streets. The havoc and harm was everywhere in the targeted district.

In the months to come, the B-29s came back three more times. By the end of May more than 50 percent of Tokyo was in ashes. The American bombardiers had tried to avoid hitting the emperor's palace. But even this building had been hit, although not seriously damaged. Millions of Tokyo residents were relocated to other cities.

Yet there was no talk of surrender. The Japanese military leaders assured the public that victory was in sight. The people believed them.

With Okinawa taken, the Americans were close to setting foot on Japan's doorstep. Yet they knew there was still a war to be won. Bombardment by planes and ships, plus deadly hand-to-hand struggles by ground troops, had brought the U.S. forces all the way to Okinawa.

If this were to continue, the first step would be weeks of bombing of the Japanese home islands. Then the big guns of American warships would have to rake the beaches for more weeks. Finally U.S. troops would have to storm ashore on landing craft and fight their way inland, yard by yard, until Japan's resistance ended.

The cost would be immense. Thousands on both sides would die. All of Japan's cities would lie in charred chaos. Its roads, farms, and power plants would be ripped apart as though struck by countless tornadoes. As a nation and a society, Japan would be destroyed.

There had to be another way. And there was.

This other way was the use of the atomic bomb. Atomic energy had only a short history. It was discovered in the late 1800s, but was regarded only as a laboratory curiosity. Then scientists realized that, properly harnessed, it had immense power to build or wipe out.

Albert Einstein, Nobel physicist, brought atomic energy and its vast potential to President Roosevelt's attention. Roosevelt needed no further prompting. He launched a crash program that turned atomic theory into a bomb that multiplied the destructive power of TNT hundreds of times over.

Colonel Tibbets and the 509th

MEANWHILE, AN aerial group was being assembled. Its ultimate mission was to drop the atomic bomb on Japan. The group first met in the summer of 1944. All kinds of military specialists attended. From their numbers the 509th Composite Group was formed. Selected as group commander was Colonel Paul Tibbets.

A tall, lean man, Tibbets, age twenty-nine, had already chalked up an impressive war record. He was one of the first to pilot a B-17 against the German Luftwaffe and had won several medals for this work. Back in the United States he helped design changes in the new B-29s just being built. Quiet but forceful, Tibbets was—despite his comparative youth—an inspiring leader.

As part of the 509th, Tibbets set up a special bombardment squadron. This was the unit that would actually drop the bomb. Tibbets staffed it with men that he knew and trusted. Training began at once over the vast and unpeopled deserts of the western United States.

From altitudes of 30,000 feet, the bombardiers released dummy bombs over white circles painted on the desert surface. The pilots practiced making sharp turns away as soon as the bombs were released. All the while the plane crews were never told about the atomic bomb or where it would be dropped. Tibbets could reveal nothing about the mission.

In the spring of 1945 the 509th was transferred to Tinian, but it was kept separate from the other bomber commands on the island. These others were still flying B-29s to bomb Japan with non-atomic explosives, and their crews wondered why the 509th was kept under wraps. But tight security was maintained.

Starting July 20, the 509th began making test flights over Japan. Twelve such dummy runs were made by July 29. Then Colonel Tibbets and the 509th settled back to await final orders.

Two weeks before, the atomic bomb had been tested at Alamogordo, New Mexico. Its devastating destructiveness astonished even the scientists and engineers who had worked on it from the beginning.

Now communications crackled between President Harry Truman (who had just succeeded Roosevelt after the President's death) and the leading statesmen in western Europe. Should the atomic bomb be used on Japan? Was its enormous destructive power too horrible even to consider using? Should it, like poison gas, be outlawed as a weapon of war?

It was President Truman, as commander-in-chief, who had to make the decision. He balanced the losses that would have occurred in an invasion of Japan against the losses brought by atom-bombing selected Japanese cities. He chose to use the bomb.

At once American planes rained millions of leaflets on Japan, warning the people of the devastation that awaited them unless they surrendered at once. The warning went unheeded. The 509th readied itself for the fateful mission.

Three planes were chosen for the actual flight. The first, carrying the bomb, was to be piloted by Colonel Tibbets. (The name painted on the B-29s nose was *Enola Gay*, after Tibbets' mother. The bomb itself was nicknamed Little Boy.)

Two other B-29s were to follow close behind. One was a camera plane to photograph the bomb damage and desolation. The other was a flying laboratory to make scientific tests of the explosion.

The day, August 6, came. The five-ton Little Boy was loaded aboard the *Enola Gay*, and the plane took off at 2:45 in the morning. The two accompanying planes followed minutes later. Fearing an accident on takeoff, the bomb experts in the *Enola Gay* did not completely assemble and arm Little Boy until they were in the air.

Two weather planes had gone on before the *Enola Gay* and its companions. Their job was to analyze the weather over several Japanese cities and report back to Colonel Tibbets. He could then choose the best target. The report was good over Hiroshima, Tibbets' first choice all along. It was Hiroshima that would suffer a cataclysmic fate.

Eighth largest city in Japan, with a population of 245,000, Hiroshima was also an important military base. It was a busy army transport center with big warehouses. It had a shipbuilding yard, textile factories, oil storage tanks, electrical utilities. Families lived in houses scattered around the industrial and military structures. Because it had been marked off early as a possible target by the 509th, Hiroshima was spared the earlier B-29 bombing missions that struck other Japanese cities.

Flying at an altitude of 31,600 feet and at a speed of 328 miles an hour, the *Enola Gay* reached Hiroshima at 8:15 in the morning. The day was bright and clear; the people were up and beginning their daily activities. Few paid any attention to the three B-29s high in the sky. The city had escaped previous bombings, and there was no reason to fear these three lone planes.

At the signal Little Boy was dropped, and Colonel Tibbets wheeled the *Enola Gay* into a sharp turn away. For an instant nothing happened. Then in a second instant a mammoth deafening roar was heard. The equivalent of 13,500 tons of TNT had exploded 1,870 feet above the ground. The roar threatened to pop the eardrums of the B-29 crews. And the light—"brighter than a thousand suns" one observer said—was blinding.

The Hiroshima poeple, caught without an idea of what was happening to them, were in their homes, out on the streets, already at their jobs. All were swept up in the roar, in the confusion, in the flames that devoured the city. Thousands were burned alive before they could take a step to safety. More thousands were killed by radiation, and still other thousands were maimed or scarred for life. A giant mushroom cloud arose from the burning city.

Dropping Little Boy caused a disaster unmatched in the age-old history of warfare. Surely Japan would now surrender, and at once. But Japan's military leaders remained silent. It was as if nothing had happened.

Perhaps Japan was gambling on the notion that the United States had only one such bomb. If so, Japan was strong enough to live through the Hiroshima holocaust and still keep on fighting. It was up to America to reinforce its first atomic strike.

On August 9, just three days after Hiroshima, a second atomic bomb (nicknamed Fat Man) was sent off to do its work. It was loaded aboard a B-29 called *Bock's Car*, which was piloted by Major Chuck Sweeney. Accompanied by two other B-29s to handle the photography and testing assignments, *Bock's Car* took off for Japan. Target: Nagasaki, a city of 200,000.

Before reaching Nagasaki, Major Sweeney ran into a series of troubles. He lost track of his photography plane. His fuel lines clogged up, slowing the fuel supply to the engines. Nevertheless he made it to Nagasaki. Fat Man fell precisely on target.

The death and devastation of Hiroshima was repeated at Nagasaki. The now-familiar mushroom cloud of smoke and flame rose above the city. Beneath it, men, women, and children were consumed by fire or felled by radiation or poisonous gases.

This time the Japanese leaders were convinced. They asked for peace on August 14 and signed the surrender papers on September 2, 1945. The war which had begun six years before was over. A quiet man named Colonel Paul

Tibbets had helped it end. The first use of atomic weapons, with their heavy and long-lasting damage, remains a controversial action even today.

And so this book ends as well. These first four decades of flight were filled with great deeds: some triumphant, some world shattering. Through the men and women who lived and died in flight, aviation and life changed in ways that would never be undone.

It has been equally so in the decades that followed: the use of jet power, the development of supersonic passenger transports, the growth of military air forces around the world. Let us hope that now air power will be employed only to keep the peace. In this book we have seen enough of war in the air.

Bibliography

Barker, A.J. *Suicide Weapon.* New York: Ballantine, 1971.
Bowen, Ezra. *Knights of the Air.* Alexandria, Va.: Time-Life Books, 1980.
Boyington, Gregory. *Baa Baa Black Sheep.* New York: Bantam, 1977.
Burlingame, Roger. *General Billy Mitchell.* New York: McGraw-Hill, 1955.
Collier, Richard. *Eagle Day.* New York: Avon, 1966.
Craig, William. *The Fall of Japan.* New York: Dial, 1967.
Fitler, Dale. *The Day the Red Baron Died.* New York: Ballantine, 1970.
Fleming, Peter. *Operation Sea Lion.* New York: Simon & Schuster, 1956.
Funderburk, Thomas P. *The Fighters.* New York: Grosset & Dunlap, 1965.
Goerner, Fred. *The Search for Amelia Earhart.* New York: Doubleday, 1966.
Inoguchi, Rikihei, and Nakajima, Tadashi. *The Divine Wind.* New York: Bantam, 1978.

Jablonski, Edward. *Airwar*. New York: Doubleday, 1971.

Jackson, Robert. *Air Heroes of World War II*. New York: St. Martin's, 1978.

Jackson, Robert. *Fighter Pilots of World War I*. New York: St. Martin's, 1977.

Klass, Joe. *Amelia Earhart Lives*. New York: McGraw-Hill, 1970.

Lawson, Don. *The United States in World War I*. New York: Scholastic, 1964.

Lawson, Don, ed. *Great Air Battles*. New York: Lothrop, 1968.

Lindbergh, Charles A. *The Spirit of St. Louis*. New York: Scribner's, 1953.

Longstreet, Stephen. *The Canvas Falcons*. New York: Ballantine, 1970.

Lyall, Gavin, ed. *The War in the Air*. London: Arrow, 1971.

Merrill, James M. *Target Tokyo*. New York: Popular Library, 1964.

Moolman, Valerie. *The Road to Kitty Hawk*. Alexandria, Va.: Time-Life Books, 1980.

Nevin, David. *The Pathfinders*. Alexandria, Va.: Time-Life Books, 1980.

Parson, Iain, ed. *The Encyclopedia of Air Warfare*. New York: Crowell, 1975.

Platt, Frank C., ed. *Great Battles of World War I*. New York: Weathervane, 1966.

Rickenbacker, Edward V. *Rickenbacker: His Own Story*. New York: Fawcett, 1967.

Ross, Walter S. *The Last Hero: Charles A. Lindbergh*. New York: Manor, 1974.

Sims, Edward H. *The Aces Talk*. New York: Ballantine, 1972.

Townsend, Peter. *Duel of Eagles*. New York: Pocket Books, 1972.
Van Wagenen, Sally Keil. *Those Wonderful Women in Their Flying Machines*. New York: Rawson, Wade, 1979.
Wallhouser, Henry T. *Pioneers of Flight*. New York: Hammond, 1969.
Whitehouse, Arch. *Heroes of the Sunlit Sky*. New York: Doubleday, 1967.
Whitehouse, Arch. *The Years of the Sky Kings*. New York: Doubleday, 1959.

Index

Aerial Experiment Association (AEA), 18, 19, 21
Airplane Contests and Prizes, 19–20, 22, 24, 27–30, 99–101, 102, 105, 106, 109, 112, 113, 120
Alcock, John, 100–102, 112
American Planes of World War I
    Curtiss Jenny, 24, 73, 77, 104
    Handley-Page, 93
    Martin, 93
American Planes of World War II
    Avenger, 144, 172
    B-17, 177
    B-25, 135, 136, 137, 138, 140, 141
    B-29 Superfort, 154, 168, 175–176, 178, 179, 180, 181
    Corsair, 144
    Curtiss P-40, 141, 142, 143
    Dauntless Dive Bomber, 144
    Hellcat, 172
    Helldiver, 172
    Lockheed Hudson Bomber, 153
    P-51 Fighter, 154
American Volunteer Group (AVG), 141, 142
Armour, J. Ogden, 28
Atomic Bomb, 177–182

Bader, Douglas, 124, 127–132, 159
Baldwin, Frederick W., 18, 19, 21
Baldwin, Thomas S., 16–17, 32
Ball, Albert, 45, 47–51, **48,** 53–54
Balloon, 12, 25, 79, 80, 81
Battle of Britain, 124–132, 159
Beachey, Lincoln, 32–33
Bell, Dr. Alexander Graham, 17–18, 19, 21
Bennett, Jim, 112–113
Berg, Edith, 147, 148
Billy Bishop Goes to War, 52
Biplane, 12, 18, 32, 56, 100
Bishop, Billy, 45, 51–55
Black Sheep Squadron, 141, 143, 145
Bock's Car, 181

Boyington, Gregory (Pappy), 141–146, **143**
British Planes of World War I
 B.E. 2c, 47, 48, 49
 Bristol Scout, 49
 De Havilland, 42, 43, 77, 91, 104
 Sopwith Camel, 43
British Planes of World War II
 Boulten Paul Defiant, 127
 Bristol Blenheim, 127
 Hurricane, 127, 129, 130, 131
 Lancaster, 162, 163, 164, 165
 Mosquito, 165
 Spitfire, 127, 131, 132
Brown, Capt. Arthur, 43–44
Brown, Arthur ("Teddie"), 100–102, 112

California Arrow, 17
Chanute, Octave, 12, 13
Chapman, Victor, 69
Chennault, Gen. Claire, 142
Churchill, Winston, 101, 126, 165
Cochran, Jacqueline, 147, 152–155, **153**
Curtiss, Glenn, 15–22, 24, 25, 32, 73

Day the Red Baron Died, The (Fitler), 44
Dickson, Capt. Bertram, 45
Dirigible, 12, 16, 17, 18, 53, 95, 96, 117–118
Doolittle, James H., 135–141, **139**
Doolittle's Raiders, 135, 168

Eagle Day (*Adler Tag*), 126, 127
Earhart, Amelia, 147, 149–151, **150,** 152

Enola Gay, 179, 180
Enterprise, 137

F-86, 155
Fighter Pilots of World War I (Jackson), 60
Flyer, 12, **14,** 15, 17, 21, 22, 147
Flying Tigers, 141, 142, 143
Fokker, Anthony, 34, 35–38, **37,** 57, 105
Fonck, René, 56, 63–66, **65**
Frantz, Joseph, 57
French Foreign Legion, 71, 73
French Planes of World War I
 Bleriot, 56, 70
 Bregeut, 56
 Caudron, 63, 73
 Deperdussin, 73
 Farman, 38, 56, 71
 Morane-Saulnier, 56, 58, 59, 60
 Nieuport, 49, 53, 54, 61, 69, 70, 71, 72, 73, 76, 78, 83, **84,** 85
 Spad, 61, 63, 76, 79, 85, 91
 Voisin, 56–57, 71

Garros, Roland, 56, 57–59
Gatty, Harold, 118, 120–122
German Luftwaffe, 125, 177
German Planes of World War I
 Albatros, 42, 53, 55, 58, 61, 72, 79, 85
 Aviatik, 57, 60, 71
 Fokker, 43, 44, 48, 49, 51, 59, 61, 69, 80, 85, 114, 115, 149
 LVG, 61
 Pfalz, 55, 85
 Rumpler, 63
 Zeppelin, 52–53, 95

188/ ACES, HEROES, AND DAREDEVILS OF THE AIR

German Planes of World War II
   Dornier, 131
   Messerschmitt, 129, 131, 132
Gibson, Guy, 158, 159–165
Glider, 12, 13
Gold Bug, 22
Göring, Hermann, 66, 110, 156
Gower, Pauline, 153
Graf Zeppelin, 118
Grahame-White, Claude, 24
Guynemer, Georges, 56, 59–63, 64

Hall, F.C., 119, 120
Hall, James Norman, 85
Halsey, Admiral William, 137
Hancock, G. Allan, 115
Hari-kiri, 167
Hawker, Major Lanoe, 42–43
Hearst, William Randolph, 27, 28, 30, 31
Henderson, 93
Herring, Augustus, 22
Hitler, Adolf, 66, 102, 110, 124, 125, 126, 156, 157
Holck, Count, 40
Hornet, 136, 137

Japanese Planes of World War II (Zero), 143, 144, 145, 169
June Bug, 19, 20, 21

Kamikaze Pilots, 169–174
Kikusui Attack, 172, 173
Kingsford-Smith, Charles, 111, 113–117, **116**
Kitty Hawk (North Carolina), 11, 12, 13, 14, 76

Layfayette Escadrille, 68–74, 81
Lansdowne, Zachary, 95–96

Le May, Gen Curtis, 175–176
Leonard, Paul, 140
Lilienthal, Otto, 12, 13
Lincoln Beachey Special, 33
Lindbergh, Charles, 66, 102–110, **108**, 149
Lockheed 10-E Electra, 151
Lockheed Vega, 74, 119
Lufbery, Raoul, 70–72, 73, 83
Luke, Frank, 75, 78–81
Lyons, Harry, 115, 117

Mars, Bud, 25–26
May, Lt. Wilfred, 44
Mitchell, Gen. William, 83, 87–98, **95**
Mitscher, Marc, 136

MacArthur, Gen. Douglas, 97
McCurdy, John, 18, 19, 21

Noonan, Fred, 151
Northcliffe, Lord, 99, 100, 101

Ohka Bomb, 172
Ohnishi, Vice-Admiral Takajiro, 168–174
Operation Sea Lion, 125
Orteig, Raymond, 102
Ostfriesland, 92–93

Pearl Harbor, 133, 134, 141, 142
Pennsylvania, 93
Pershing, Gen. John J., 72, 90, 91
Piper Cub, 148
Post, Wiley, 111, 118–123
Pourpé, Marc, 70–71, 72
Prince, Norman, 68–70, 71, 74

Quenault, Louis, 56–57
Quimby, Harriet, 148–149

INDEX /189

Red Baron. *See* Von Richthofen, Baron Manfred.
Red Wing, 18, 19
Reitsch, Hanna, 147, 156–157
Rickenbacker, Capt. Edward, 75, 81–86, **84,** 145
Roberts, Ivan, 80
Rodgers, Calbraith Perry, 26–32
Rogers, Will, 123
Roosevelt, Eleanor, 153, 154
Roosevelt, President Franklin, 97, 110, 134, 177, 178
Royal Air Force, 45, 51, 114, 128, 129, 142, 143, 159, 161, 165

Rubber Cow, 32
Ryan Airlines, 106

Saint Lo, 170
Santos-Dumont, Albert, 58
Scientific American, 15, 19, 20, 22
Seki, Lt. Yukio, 169, 170
Selfridge, Lt. Thomas, 18, 19, 21
Shenandoah, 95–96
Shiers, Wally, 112–113
Shimpu Attack Unit, 169
Silver Dart, 21
Smith, Keith, 112–113
Smith, Ross, 111, 112–113
Southern Cross, 114, 115, **116,** 117
Spirit of St. Louis, The, 106, 107, **108**
Storks Squadron, 62, 63, 64, 80
Sweeney, Major Chuck, 181

Thaw, Bill, 73–74
Tibbets, Col. Paul, 177–182
Trenchard, Major General Hugh, 90

Truman, President Harry, 178–179

Ulm, Charles, 114–115, 117
U.S. Air Force, 88, 94, 134
U.S. Army Air Corps, 153, 154
U.S. Signal Corps, 72, 89, 90

Vickers Vimy, 100, 112, 113
Vin-Fiz Flyer, 29, 30, 31
Von Greim, Colonel-General Ritter, 156, 157
Von Richthofen, Lothar, 39, 43, 51
Von Richthofen, Baron Manfred ("The Red Baron"), 34, 38–44, **42,** 50–51, 66

Wallis, Dr. Barnes, 160, 161, 163
Warner, James, 115, 117
Wehner, Joe, 80
White Wing, 19
Wilson, President Woodrow, 75, 76
Winnie Mae, 119, 120, 121, 122, 123
Wisseman, Capt. Kurt, 63
Women's Airforce Service Pilots (WASP), 152–155
World War I, 23, 24, 26, 34–86, 87, 88, 99, 103, 104, 111, 112, 145
World War II, 66, 86, 88, 93, 110, 112–146, 152–157, 158–182
Wright-Bellance, 105
Wright, Orville, 11–15, **14,** 16, 17, 18, 20, 21, 22, 24, 27, 28, 34, 99
Wright, Wilbur, 11–15, **14,** 16, 17, 18, 20, 21, 22, 24, 27, 28, 34, 99, 147–148

ABOUT THE AUTHOR

Aces, Heroes, and Daredevils of the Air is LeRoy Hayman's eleventh book for young people, his third under the Julian Messner imprint. The first two were *Thirteen Who Vanished* (1979) and *Up, Up, and Away!* (1980). He has been a college teacher and editor of both young people's encyclopedias and magazines.

Hayman was a junior officer in the U.S. Navy during World War II. He has lived in Chicago and New York and now makes his home in south Florida. Despite the lure of the sun and sea, Hayman does a daily stint at his typewriter.

"For much of my working life, I've written and edited for young people," Hayman says. "I'm read because I take my audience seriously. This present book will be fun to read. But it will also satisfy my audience's need to know the real world about them. If it gives my readers an insight into what makes a flier tick, then I've done my job."